Claimed

Claimed

The Shadow and Light Heritage

Rebecca Hendrix

Labyrinth Press

ISBN: 979-8-9941190-0-6
Library of Congress Control Number: 2025925836

Published by Labyrinth Press · Roy, Utah

Printed in the United States of America.
First Edition 2025

Cover Design: Ashley Conrad

This is a work of fiction. Names, characters, places, and incidents either originate from the author's imagination or are used fictitiously. Any resemblance to actual persons, living or dead, or actual events is purely coincidental.

For information, permissions, or inquiries, contact:
Labyrinth Press / Rebecca Hendrix, Author

LABYRINTH
PRESS

For all my family; on both sides of the veil.

Always.

"All men know that they must die… and it is a subject we ought to study more than any other. We ought to study it day and night, for the world is ignorant in reference to their true condition and relation."

-Joseph Smith

Chapter 1

The streets were bright. Warm and bright. While it hadn't been long, (or had it been?) Martha was used to it. More than used to it; she found she always had longed for it, and it was beautiful. Everything she'd ever known to be good was nothing compared to how her life was now. Could it be called a life? She'd have to ask sometime. Complete was the only word she could think of to fully encompass her emotions. As she walked down the street, she knew she should be in more of a hurry, but she relished the moment and walked slowly to savor all her surroundings. Everything shone with such brilliance in the sun, and she wondered how anyone could live without wanting to experience this beauty around them. The sidewalk seemed to glow where a small dandelion peeked out from a crack. Her eyes subconsciously followed the crack where it continued down the curb and only ended once the concrete met the blacktop of the road. The stark contrast between the dark street and the bright cement called her mind to her grandfather. A moment of deep grief welled up inside her, but she knew he wouldn't be happy here. She pressed the thought from her mind and kept walking forward. A love filled her - and slowly helped to fade the grief that had snuck up on her - each time she passed someone on the street, and she knew they felt it when she smiled at them.

As she continued down the street, the sound of her feet on the sidewalk was crisp as she stepped purposefully toward the large house on the corner of block ahead. Each house she passed had the look of rushed construction and lack of individuality, but she knew the people who lived inside them must have infinitely unique histories. The air was refreshing, and she could feel it whispering past her as she progressed toward her destination. Sweet and fresh, the air filled her with joy and anticipation of her task at hand. When she was presented with the opportunity to help Amanda, she jumped at the chance. Amanda had been working tirelessly to help so many around her, selflessly working with no thanks and no expectation of reward. When Amanda had helped Martha, she was especially grateful. Martha had felt lost for so long and when Amanda had offered to help her, she had no idea what that truly meant to her. This was a small way for Martha to help Amanda in return.

Absorbed in thoughts of gratitude and memories, Marhta almost didn't realize she had reached Amanda's home. The blue siding of the house rose two stories and culminated in a black shingled roof, just like the other houses on this street. The doors of the balcony on the second floor were open to cool the interior of the house and get some reprieve from the heat of the previous week. The smell of the changing leaves was welcoming and restorative. As Martha stepped onto the porch, she heard a whimper from upstairs. Cayson, Amanda's toddler, had been teething for a while and he hadn't been handling it well at all. Things got worse when his simple teething discomfort turned into a double ear infection within the last day, and he was so miserable which in turn, made Amanda miserable and exhausted. This was why Martha had been called to help her. Amanda's overly tired body and depleted mental energy were draining, and she desperately needed a hand. Amanda never complained or asked for anyone's help, but Martha knew she needed it. Amanda's Husband, Jason was the one who had plead for help for his wife. He knew that Amanda needed help and was too worried about bothering others or being a burden to ask for it for herself, though Martha knew she would be grateful for it if it were offered. While Martha had never directly talked with either Amanda or Jason, she knew exactly what she was here to do. She stood on the porch as she listened to Cayson's whimper turn to a full outcry as Amanda tried to sooth him with the usual motherly "shushing" which turned to humming and then to singing which seemed to calm the little one. He was still having a hard time taking regular breaths in between his, now subsiding, cries. Martha heard the subtle creak of a rocking chair accompanying the soft lullaby. Martha let herself in, not wanting to disrupt Amanda or her sweet little one who just started calming down.

Once inside, Martha walked through the kitchen and then downstairs to the unfinished basement. The large space was roughly sectioned off into quarters. One quarter was packed from floor to ceiling shelves filled with canned goods and other food necessities as well as cleaning supplies and toiletries. Another corner was dedicated to what looked like an abundance of holiday decorations and lesser used lawn ornaments and outdoor games. The third space was set up a makeshift office/play area/craft studio. This was where Amanda and Jason worked while Cayson played near them. A large, soft, and springy cushion lay on the floor of this area, a computer desk on one side and a craft table on the other. A small bin of toys next to a basket full of blankets were in the center of the rug. A small love seat was on the edge of the rug, its back creating a division from the rest of the basement and creating a small but happy space in which they could work together as a family when needed.

In the last section of the basement the walls were lined with mismatched shelves. Boxes littered the floor. Some in piles stacked neatly, but most were haphazardly strewn around the vicinity. This was the "junk" spot. The place where things went to be dealt with later. The place where things would go that just couldn't be dealt with right now. Jason jokingly called it "The 'Graveyard.' Because that's where things went to die and were forgotten." Martha had personal reasons to be glad that wasn't the case. This fourth and last area of the basement was where she would be working.

A year ago, Amanda's grandmother had died and left her everything. Amanda was her only living descendant and while Amanda was grateful, she had been overwhelmed by the prospect of going through everything with a small baby in tow. She had spent the better part of three months going through her grandmother's house and cleaning it. Amanda's grandmother was a hoarder and of the worst kind. On the plus side, Amanda had recently gotten into genealogy and her Grandmother had never allowed anyone to even look at what she had in relation to family history. Amanda's mother had been an avid genealogist and worked for one of the largest genealogical libraries in the world. She had longed to delve into the myriad boxes of historical things that Amanda's grandmother had claimed lay in the cluttered house, though grandmother wouldn't even let her own daughter through the front door, worried she would steal everything. As a result, Amanda had never visited her grandmother's house while she was still alive. Grandma would always come and visit them, and Amanda had a beautiful relationship with her. Amanda's mother would often say, "As soon as Grandma dies, I'm taking all that history home with me and burning the rest." When Amanda started the arduous process of cleaning the house, she understood the sentiment and wished that her own mother had still been alive to help with this emotionally, mentally, and physically demanding task.

Fortunately, while the house was full of everything from old books to computers, piles of garbage and boxes containing things like expired food or family history things, it was all organized into sections. One small bedroom was full of garbage and mouse droppings and nothing else. Another room was filled with printed works, from books to magazines. Newspapers to flyers. Sheet Music and recipe cards. Most of the books were donated to the local library and thrift stores. There was a large closet next to the kitchen that had, Amanda guessed, originally been meant as a large walk-in pantry, but was where all of Grandma's family history stuff was. There were at least forty file boxes labeled "Genealogy" or "Family" or "Historically significant". By the time everything was said and done the only thing Amanda could do was take all the boxes home and put them downstairs in the "Graveyard". And here all the boxes still sat almost a year later, largely untouched.

Amanda knew there were a few boxes full of pictures and old photographs among them. She was hoping to find one specific picture of a long-lost cousin of Amanda's; one Amanda had stumbled upon while dabbling in some old family history stuff her mother had left her when she had unexpectantly passed away five years before grandma died. She felt drawn to this cousin whom she had never met or known and wanted to know as much as she could about her and her family. It had taken Amanda nearly three years to learn all that she had about her cousin and had hoped against hope that she could find a photo of said cousin among the thousands of articles hidden inside these boxes. This was what Martha was here to help with. This was what Amanda needed the most at this moment. Finding this photograph, Martha new, would bring a deep well of peace to Amanda that she could draw on in the coming months, in spite of all the chaos and everything going on with her personal life.

Amanda needed this picture of her cousin so she could mentally close that chapter and focus on the upcoming changes in her family's life.

Martha sat on the ground and pulled the closest box to her. Inside she found letters, letters and more letters. The next box had more letters but also some newspaper clippings regarding the family who'd also written those letters. More boxes, more letters. Some photos and some family memorabilia. An occasional trophy or medal. One box made Martha's heart leap when she saw what was in it; a war medal for someone who'd served in the army. Emotions flared within her chest.

Chapter 2

Fourteen -year-old Martha, her black shoes (which had been lovely and shined that morning) were caked brown with sticky mud. Her socks were no longer anywhere near white, and she didn't even care. She just stared at her own feet as she walked down the dirt road with May, her best friend.

May was everything good in this world and a stark contrast to her own self that was, as Suzie put it so clearly today, "Everything that was ever wrong with anyone." She wasn't sure Suzie was wrong. Martha was quite different from every other girl in school. Her dark mess of curly hair was always everywhere no matter what she or her mother tried to do with it. She never seemed to have quite as nice things as anyone else. It was mostly handed down to her from May. Not that she minded. May and Martha were almost the same age, just a few months apart, but May was a good eight inches taller than Martha, so it made sense to both their mothers to let the clothes be well used instead of tossed away when they "Still had so much life in them."

The mud was caked on her shoes and made it difficult to walk in a straight line without tripping. Both girls had dust and mud from their toes to their knees. The walk home from school was never a clean one, but the sporadic rain the last few days had made many mud puddles, some were large enough to be unavoidable, but the flat ground was now dry and dusty, making it impossible to stay clean. Martha grimaced as Scott, the oldest of May's four younger brothers, ran hard and fast to catch up to them, then jumped heavily into the closest muddy puddle, splattering both girls all over their left sides in mud, even into their hair. Deryk, Grayson, and Morgan laughed loudly as they ran faster to catch up to their brother, splashing in the puddle as well.

"Stop it!" May shouted with indignation, "Mary's had a horrid day already without you lot getting us all muddied! Mama will NOT be happy to hear about this!" May was always so kind to her, she loved her for it. May reached for Martha's hand and squeezed it. The boys all laughed loudly and ran faster down the lane leaving the girls to finish walking home alone.

"Thanks." Martha mumbled as she tried to force a smile up at her friend.

"Do you want to talk about it?" May said squeezing her hand.

"No. Not really." She reclaimed her own hand and hugged herself tightly.

"Suzie's just mean! Ignore her. She's just jealous because she isn't as pretty as you are."

She knew May meant well, and it was true that Suzie wasn't very fortunate in appearance as most girls were, but she hadn't teased Martha for weeks now about her looks. She had started becoming ruthless toward Martha for no apparent reason. She used to poke fun of anyone who wasn't one of her three close friends, if you could call her small group friends. Martha and May and the boys all suspected that the other two girls that played with Suzie only hung around her to prevent her from picking on them, but the last few days in particular, Martha had become Suzie's favorite victim and would go out of her way to only pick on her. And today, in earnest. At lunch, Suzie had gotten another girl to trick her into going to the edge of the grass, once she was there, the girl ran away, looking terrified. Suzie had stepped out from behind a tree and said the meanest things she had ever said to anyone, then ran off laughing.

No one else had heard what she had said to Martha, but she knew that within the next week the whole school would know. And then, no one would look at her or talk to her. Scott, Deryk, Grayson and Morgan might not even talk to her again. Maybe not even May, her best friend. Thoughts of being forever lonely stopped her breath and she couldn't take another step forward. Thoughts turned to fear.

"Mary!" May had stopped walking too and had grabbed her arm. "MARY, BREATHE!" She commanded. Martha gasped as she realized she probably hadn't been breathing for at least a minute. Tears filled her eyes then quickly spilled over. There was no stopping them now.

"No matter what you hear next week at school," Martha sputtered between sobs, "promise me you'll still be my friend?" Martha held her breath again, waiting for the answer.

"Oh!" was all May could say. Without another word, she stepped in close to Martha, wrapped her arms tight around her and started crying too. It was a whole minute before Martha could bring her arms up and hug her back. Both girls crying so hard, their shoulders shook. May took Martha by the shoulders, firmly but with so much love in her eyes, there was no doubt she was telling the truth.

"Martha Rose Jones. I have never been your friend!" a moment of panic, "For you have always been the sister I was missing! I can't ever be less than that to you. No matter what anyone says, no matter what you ever do, you'll always, AL-WAYS be my sister!" Martha hugged her back, tighter than before.

"Promise?"

"Of course! I don't know… I mean, I can guess…. But…" May pulled away, "We really should be getting home. Mama will get worried when I don't walk in with the boys."

Martha started walking after her, grabbing her hand and as she caught up with her, "But what, May? But what?"

Their feet crunched the loose gravel on the short stretch of dry ground before May finally replied. "Mama won't be happy if I say." May looked as though she might say it anyway but then shook her head. "But I do promise that no matter what I hear, you'll always be my best friend. My best friend AND my sister."

"What is it, May?" Martha released May's hand for the second time and stood with clenched fists at her sides. May turned to look at her but stood in silence.

After a long time, Martha sat down right where she was, before she realized that she was standing in a small mudpuddle. She didn't care that her bottom was getting wet with the muddy water. She wouldn't move until May said what she almost let slip. May knew it too, because she walked back to her and sat next to her, also getting muddy all over her rear.

"I really can't. I promised Mama I wouldn't say any-thing. But I will tell you that I'm pretty sure I know what Suzie said to you, and I understand why you don't want to talk about it. But I do think you need to talk to your mother. Tell her what Suzie said and ask her why. When we get back home, I'll tell mama not to expect you two for dinner to-night, and I'll make sure cook brings you both something hot to eat." May stood, brushed herself off as best she could and reached a hand down to Martha. She took it and reluctantly, half in shock then stood and continued walking hand in hand with May until they reached the front of the large property that held both their homes. They paused at the start of the long driveway, May turned and hugged Martha again, "Go to your mother, tell her everything. I promise I'll still be here, and I also promise you'll be ok. We can talk about it later if you want to. But… if after you talk to your mama and you still don't want to talk about it with me, that's ok too!"

Martha stood stiff as she looked up at the large house, wishing she could just pretend nothing had happened, that everything was the same as it had been that morning. May's figure shrank as she walked up the front walk to the steps and into her house. Martha looked at the large open yard, took a deep breath and walked around the house, slowly, enjoying the soft grass and trying to let the gentle breeze that remained from the last patchy storm blow away her anxiety. The property of May's family was quite extensive, and the massive Victorian house and main yard were on nearly a full acre alone. Near the very back of the main yard was a small, one-bedroom house. There was a kitchen, a bathroom and even a small sitting room. May's father had put up a little white picket fence around the tiny building before Martha had learned to walk. She didn't remember it happening, but her mother had reminded her often that it was so kind of him to put it up for them, because Martha was able to hold on to the fence and walk all around the house without her mother fearing she'd wander into the small creek on the property.

Her breath caught in her throat again and tears threatened to return. She had noticed her life was different than most girls her age, but she hadn't really thought about how different it really was until today when Suzie had been so blatant and mean about it. This was the only life she'd ever known and as far as she could tell, it was a good life!

She was happy. She never really wanted or stood in need of anything. She knew she was loved. She had her mama, and a loving Aunt and Uncle. Mr. and Mrs. Clark weren't really her aunt and uncle, she knew that, but she'd always called them that. They loved her like a niece, and they didn't have any real nieces or nephews, so they were always happy when she called them such. Mama worked for Mrs. Clark, who Martha called, Aunt Ruth. Mama was their housekeeper and gardener. But Mama and she were always treated more like family, though standing here now, she realized she never knew how she and her mother came to be here.

With a sigh heavier than any 14-year-old had ever released, she opened the small gate on the white picket fence and approached the tiny house. The front door felt unnaturally heavy as it opened with a foreboding squeak that was followed by silence.

"Mama?" She was proud of how steady her voice was although she was now shaking with years of unanswered questions. Questions she never realized she had. The sitting room was neat and clean, the small armchair in the corner was worn but well-loved and comfortable, her mother's book resting on the seat waiting to be finished. The small sofa on the opposite side of the room with a small coffee table in front of it. A bookshelf was along another wall with a few books and mementos from Martha's infancy. The room was empty besides. Through the door on the far side of the room, she heard her mother reply, "I'm in the bedroom." Martha followed her mother's voice.

The bedroom wasn't big, but it held a dresser on one wall and two twin sized beds with a nightstand between them and a lamp on top. Mama was folding a basket of laundry, Martha sat on the edge of her bed, hoping her mother wouldn't turn and look at her while she talked. Wishing she would just keep her back to her and keep at her task while she spoke, it would be easier than having to look at her and have this conversation. Not once in her whole life had mama ever mentioned Martha's father and for some reason Martha had never thought to ask. Until now.

"Mama", there was now a quiver in Martha's voice that was uncontrollable, and she could feel traitorous tears escaping her eyes. Her mother must have heard the desperation in her single word, for she immediately dropped the skirt she was holding and turned with concern and so much love on her face that Martha nearly didn't want to ask what she knew she needed to ask. Nearly.

Her mother's face was sweet, heart-shaped and pale with a few freckles on her cheeks, her long curly dark hair bounced as she turned, it was unruly and always pulled half back to keep it out of her face. One thing she and Mama had in common was all that hair.

"What's happened?" Worry filling her face as she stepped over to sit on the bed next to her.

"Suzie", was all Martha could mutter. Her mother knew how awful Suzie could be to people, so instead of responding, she just nodded, with understanding and encouragement on her face, silently urging her daughter to continue.

"She said no one would ever want to talk to me again once they all knew I didn't even have a father."

Comprehension flooded her mother's face and what seemed to be a flash of pain that quickly turned to grief then determination. She nodded and waited for Martha to continue.

"I never really thought much about it until today, but I must have had a father… right?"

Her mother took a deep breath, then shifted slightly so she could hold Martha's hands, and looked down at their entwined fingers as she gently rubbed the back of her daughter's hands, speaking slowly at first.

"Martha Rose Jones," her mother only used her full name when she was angry or very concerned for her daughter, every other time it was Mary, "of course, you had a father." Mama thought for a moment, "You have a father." Another pause and Mama's face was thoughtful now. "I've never wanted to keep the truth from you, but I thought I needed to wait until you came to me with the questions. It's kind of a heavy load and I never wanted to burden you." The briefest glimpse of pain seemed to flash in Mama's eyes, then it was gone. "What do you want to know?"

What did she want to know? From never thinking about the man to suddenly having so many questions she didn't know how to put into words was a lot for a ten-year-old. She thought for a moment then they started spilling out so fast she couldn't quite control them. "Who is he? Where is he? Did he not love me? Did he stop loving you? Did he die? Is he dead? How did he die?" Martha paused when she noticed Mama's eye got big at the explosion of words and realized she'd been rambling. Martha took a deep breath before she continued, "I guess I want to know everything. Suzie made it sound like you were… well, as if you weren't, um… she used a not nice word." Martha settled. "Were you two married?"

A small smile stole briefly across her mother's face quickly replaced with a somber and still set mouth.

"Yes, we were married. I don't think your father is dead… though I can't honestly say for sure. The last time I spoke to him was when you were in my belly."

"What happened? Did he not want us?"

"Let me start at the beginning, my dear, sweet girl." She shifted again on the bed and wrapped her arms around Martha, took a steadying breath and spoke softly. "When I was 14 my younger sister, Angela, got very sick. She was just 10 years old, the same age as you are now, but the doctors couldn't do anything for her. My parents tried everything they could, but she just kept getting sicker and sicker no matter how many doctors they took her to. She died. About a year later, my parents had lost everything. They'd sold everything they could to pay for the hospital visits trying to save Angela. It also broke them. Before she got sick, they were very good parents to Angie, James and I."

"WAIT!" Martha interrupted, her head spinning. "I have an aunt and an uncle too?" She had assumed she had a father at some point but truly hadn't ever entertained the thought that she'd have other family members too.

"Yes, I guess I never talked to you about any of my family." Mama said with a pout "I'm sorry for that, but I hope you'll forgive me once you hear the whole story. I was the oldest, then James was next. Angela was the baby."

"I'm sorry your sister died, Mama. That's so sad!" Martha's eyes began to water again, but just before the first tear could fall, Mama wiped it away.

"Yes, it was very sad. I still sometimes cry because I miss her so much." Mama wiped at her own eye now, "It was so hard on all of us, it nearly killed my mother too. She was never the same after Angie died. She became a completely different person and didn't care to be around any of us much.

It was like my mother died with Angie. There were a lot of not nice things she ended up saying and doing, but I will just say that home wasn't a safe place for me anymore."

"Oh, Mama!" Martha was trying to wrap her head around all of this. "What about your father? What happened to him after she died?"

"Well," Mama said scooting closer to Martha and putting an arm around her shoulders. "He, your grandfather, and my brother, your uncle James, were my safe space and the only thing that kept me from falling apart. Oh, they would love you! But my father couldn't always keep me safe from my mother. He still had a job and was trying his best to keep a roof over our heads and food on the table when Mama was losing her mind. I know it must have been difficult him watching his family fall apart like that."

"So," Martha interrupted, "what happened then?"

"After a few years, when I was old enough but still very young, I met your father, William." Mama looked far away for a moment. Then whispered, "Will." She breathed a heavy sigh before she continued. "William's father, your other grandfather, wasn't a kind man at all. He made my mother, on her worst days, look like a saint. He never loved any of us and looked at William as though he had ruined his whole life. William's mother loved him very much. She was the kindest, sweetest lady you'd ever meet."

Martha hung on every word her mother was saying. She couldn't believe there were so many people who were her family. So many people who were part of her that she never knew about. People she'd never thought about! Her mother had stopped speaking and was looking out the bedroom window that looked out over the back part of the property that went down into a small, wooded area where the stream flowed. The window was open, and the trickle of water brought a sort of peace and comfort to the room. Martha realized that her anxiety had long since dissipated and she was calm now. But what about her father, William? She hadn't learned nearly anything about him yet.

"How did you meet my father?" Martha probed.

"Well, let's just say that my father helped me find him so that I could get out of the house and away from my mother and not be in danger anymore."

"Oh." Martha said, deflating suddenly. Her heart sank and she felt the room begin to spin.

"What is it, Mary?" Her mother asked as she cupped her daughter's chin gently and lifted her eyes to her own.

"I don't know." Martha paused. "Would it have been better if you and my father hadn't been married?"

"Why do you say that?" Mother let go of her chin and pulled her into her lap. Nothing but love between them.

"Because," Martha continued, "at least you would have loved each other. It's horrible that you had to marry just to leave your parents' house."

"Oh, my sweet, sweet girl," mama held her close and brushed some unruly curls away from her face, "we loved each other very much."

"You did?" Martha felt a rush of hope again.

"Oh yes." Mama got a faraway look in her eyes. "It all felt like a fairy tale come true."

"Really?" Martha couldn't help her excitement. She scooted off Mother's lap and knelt on the bed, only then remembering how muddy she was. "I'm so sorry mama." She looked down and saw mud and dirt all over the floor, her mother and the bed.

"Don't you worry at all. It can be cleaned later; this is far more important."

Martha looked up at her mother and wished that she could be as kind as she was. "Are you sure?"

"Yes, I'm sure." Mama smiled warmly, a full smile that reached not only her eyes but all the way to her ears.

"Was it really like a fairy tale?" Martha's heart was racing now, she had to know everything about her father.

"Yes, it was!" Mama smiled from ear to ear, "The moment I met William, it was as if I'd stumbled upon the most beautiful man that ever existed. Come to think of it, I still think he's the most beautiful man I've ever seen. In fact, you have his eyes."

"I do?" Martha exclaimed in delight.

"Yes, ma'am." Mama replied as she reached for a small mirror that was on the nightstand.

Martha looked at her mother and then herself in the mirror. She'd never paid much attention to her own looks before but now realized just how much she looked like her mother. They could almost be identical, except her nose and her eyes were very different. She looked back at mother, then back at the mirror.

"Are they really my father's eyes?" Martha asked, uncertain. Mother had big beautiful brown eyes, hers were very blue and while they were large, they were more almond shaped than Mama's.

"Oh yes." Mama assured her. "Very much your father's eyes."

"Is my nose his too?" Martha asked looking one last time in the mirror before handing it back to mama.

"No, that nose is actually my mother's, who I named you after." Mama said, taking the mirror and placing it back on the nightstand. "You are Martha, after my mother Martha. Rose, after my sister, Angela Rose. You have your father's eyes and my mother's nose."

"If your mama was so mean, why did you name me after her?"

"Because," mama paused, "she wasn't always mean. She used to be incredibly wonderful. Sometimes when someone goes through something incredibly painful, it can change them. I named you after the wonderful mother I used to know. I try not to think of the awful mother I had later in life, because I loved the first mother I had so much. Does that make sense?"

Martha thought for a moment, "I think so."

"Anyway," Mama began again, "I met your father and immediately liked him. He was so sweet and gentle, and he liked me just as much as I liked him. He was strong and brave. He served in the army too. By the time we were married I had never trusted anyone more than him and had no idea I could love anyone so much. After we got married, we were so happy. His mother took me in and loved me just as wonderfully as my own mother had before she had lost her hope. Will's mother was so important to him, and he meant everything to her. Unfortunately, she died not too long after we were married. That broke your father as much as losing Angie broke my mother. He didn't know how to manage his anger and his grief and when his own father wasn't a good example of how to be a good husband even when you're hurting, he didn't have much to look to sadly. He got mean too. Unlike my mother however, he honestly felt terrible after he'd have an episode of unkindness. And I hoped it would pass. Time went by and most days he was the man I knew and loved, only sometimes was he different and unkind.

"Then, I found out I was pregnant with you! I was so excited to tell your father. I'd hoped that you would be a little bit of a healing balm for his broken heart. But that same night he came home meaner than I'd ever seen him…" mama broke off and stood to face the window. A long time went by before she spoke again. Martha couldn't see her face but when Mama reached up to wipe her cheek, she knew she'd been crying.

"Are you alright, Mama" Martha asked, concerned.

"Yes, my darling." Mama wiped her cheeks again but didn't look at Martha. "well, I knew it wasn't safe to stay there with you inside me, growing. I was worried we'd both be hurt if I stayed. I left and came here. Your aunt and uncle took me in when no one else would. They gave me a family when I didn't have anyone else."

"What about your father? Your brother?" asked Martha.

"I don't know what happened to my brother. After I married, he had no reason to stay. I suspect he left home one day and just never came back. Mama wouldn't give him my letters or accept any of my visits or calls. He had no idea where to find me so we never saw each other again after I married Will. After I left Will to keep you safe, I tried my mother. I was going to tell her I was pregnant and in danger but when she saw me, she didn't want anything to do with me, when I asked to see my father, she told me he had died too."

"So, we have no one then." Martha said, it wasn't a question.

"We have Ruth and Daniel. We have May, Scott, Deryk, Grayson and Morgan. We have wonderful neighbors. You have an amazing teacher and," Mama finally turned to look at her, "most importantly we have each other." Mama, with red, tear burned eyes, held her arms out for Martha.

Martha climbed off the bed, dried clumps of mud clambered to the floor, but instead of being upset it made Mama smile, and she wrapped her arms tightly around Martha the moment she was within reach.

"Mama?"

"Yes?"

"So, my father doesn't even know about me?"

"I don't suspect so. I hadn't told anyone at all, only the doctor knew."

"Do you think," Martha paused, uncertain if she really wanted to know the answer, "do you think he would have liked me?"

Mama squeezed her tighter. "Oh yes, he certainly would have loved you dearly."

"Mama?"

"Hmm?"

"I wonder… would he want me now?"

"I believe he would."

"Do you think he's still… unkind?"

"I don't honestly know." Mama got quiet for a while again. Martha didn't dare say anything else. She just waited for Mama to speak. After a minute or more of only being able to hear the stream and the birds through the window, she squeezed Mama tight to see if it would prompt anything further. Mama inhaled sharply and continued, "I think I'm too afraid to find out. I still love him with all my heart. He's still my husband and I want him in my life. But if I were to return to him and he was still broken inside his heart, I wouldn't be able to find the strength to leave again but I could never go back if there was even the smallest chance that it could mean hurting you. I will never put you in harm's way for my own selfishness."

"You love him that much?" Martha had to ask.

"I do," Mama replied, "I love you that much too. That's why we are here."

"If you love him that much, how do you stay away?"

"I tell myself that he's dead. I don't know if it's true or not, but if he's alive and I can't be with him it hurts more than if he's gone and I can't be with him. I don't know if I'm making mistakes by being here or not, but I do know we are safe here. We have a beautiful life and watching you grow into such a lovely young woman is everything I could hope for."

"William Jones." Martha tried the name.

"What?" Mama asked.

"William Jones, my father's name. I just wanted to say it once." Martha said.

Mother let go of her then and turned and sat on the bed, burying her face in her hands.

"I'm sorry, Mama." Martha went to her mother's side and put a hand on her shoulder. "I won't say it again."

"No, it isn't that."

"What is it?"

"No, it isn't that. That isn't his name."

"His name isn't William?"

"It is. His name is William." Mama paused again, took a deep breath then looked up from her hands and into Martha's eyes. "It's William Hart."

"Hart?"

"Yes, I was honestly worried he might try to find me, so I called our last name Jones when I came here and had you."

"William Hart?" Martha whispered, worried it would make mama cry again, but it didn't. Mama smiled warmly.

"Yes. Hart. You're a Hart. You're a Hart and a Loudry. That was my last name before we got married."

"Thank you, Mama." Martha bent to hug her mother and didn't let go for a long time.

"For what?" Mama said from within the strangling hug.

"Thank you for telling me about my family. Now I can tell that awful Suzie you are married and that I do have a father."

"Oh, Mary." Mama said, pulling Martha's arms from around her neck, then grasping her shoulders firmly. "You can never tell anyone. It could be very dangerous."

"I know mama." Martha smiled knowingly. "I'm Martha Rose Jones. But I can say that you were married, and that my father died after you became pregnant with me."

Another tear rolled down her mother's cheek, as Mama released her shoulders Martha wiped the tear away.

"Thank you, my sweet girl. I love you so much and I'm so sorry you're caught in the middle of all of this."

"Thank you, Mama, for doing what you needed to so you could keep us safe." She hugged Mama again. She didn't fully understand why Mama had to leave her father to be safe, but she understood the emotion and fear she saw in her mother's face. She knew her mother loved her father and could sense the deep conflict Mama had between loving him and keeping her daughter safe, and most of all, Martha knew her mother loved her. She could respect and accept her decision.

After a while there was a soft knock on the door. While Mama regained her composure, Martha opened the front door. The Clark's cook, Mrs. Anderson, stood on the small porch. She was a kindly old woman. Her hair was completely grey though her face didn't look too wrinkled with time. Her eyes held all her years within them and only a few seemed to spill out of those ancient blues onto the lids and skin around them. She smiled warmly when she saw Martha, and her grin made the deep laugh lines in her dark skinned face feel like home.

"I thought you two could use a quiet dinner here together." She said holding out a large plate in her hands and a small sack over one arm. The plate brought with it the very smell of life. Fresh steamed broccoli and baked chicken. In the sack, Martha could smell hot fresh rolls.

"Thank you." Martha said, Mrs. Anderson gave her the plate, and the sack then walked back to the large main house. Marth turned and took the meal to the table in the small kitchen. As she set the food down, Mama walked into the room and pulled plates and glasses from the cupboard. They set the table in silence, clinking glasses and rattling forks, the only thing breaking up the quiet. It wasn't peaceful, though neither of them spoke as they ate. Martha could feel the weight of the unspoken words between them. Yes, she could and would respect her mother's decision. She knew everything she had said was true, she never knew her mother to be dishonest or act in any way selfishly. So, what she had been told had to be true, but Martha also sensed that something had changed, and she knew her mother could tell that Martha had more questions, though she was now afraid to ask them. What exactly had her father done that had warranted such an outcome? Martha's mother's father was gone, and her father's mother too. What about her other grandparents, were they still alive? Mother had described her grandfather as unkind in every way and her grandmother unkind as well, at least since Mother's sister had died. What about her uncle? Was he still alive? So many questions rattled inside her head, Martha couldn't look up from her plate at her mother. She wasn't sure what to do with any of the information she had received. This new knowledge helped somewhat; it would likely stop Suzie from picking on her from now on. Suzie's own father had died a few years ago. Everyone else in class knew it, and no one else had lost a parent before. Martha didn't expect that even Suzie could possibly be that mean.

Once dinner was finished and the table was cleared, the sun had long since set and the landscape outside the window was all dark and still. Mama sent Martha off to get ready for bed while she cleaned the dishes. School started "early tomorrow, and you need your sleep."

Martha readied for bed, and by the time she got to the bedroom she saw Mama was just finishing making her bed with clean sheets and a clean blanket after the muddy mess she had made. The rest of the room was clean too. How had Mama cleaned everything so fast? How long had she taken to get ready for bed? Martha's mind was still racing, and she couldn't stop it. She wanted to thank her mama, but no words would come, so she just stood near the door uncertain what to say. Mama hadn't seen her walk into the room. When Mama had finished with the bed she stood and saw Martha, she too didn't say anything, but she did smile, a sad half smile that still showed all the love she had for her only child. She turned again to the bed and turned down the covers. Martha walked over to the bed and wrapped her arms around her mother. Eyes closed, she squeezed her mother's waist as tightly as she could, trying to communicate all her emotions in the gesture. She loved her mother. She wanted her to know how truly grateful she was to her, and she needed her to know that she would also love her forever, no matter what. But Martha could tell that something had irrevocably changed between them. Her whole life, it had just been her and Mama. They had Aunt Ruth, they had Uncle Daniel, they had May and the boys. But it truly had been just her and Mama. Always. They had relied on each other for everything. As her mother hugged her back, Martha fought hard against the tears. She would not let them fall until she was in bed. She slowly released her mother and looked up at her, Mama looked down and kissed Martha's forehead. Soft and gentle, gentler that she had ever been, Martha hoped her eyes hadn't betrayed her emotions the same way Mama's did in that moment that they looked at each other. Martha let go of Mama and climbed into bed as Mama covered her up and tucked her in. Martha still wanted to say, 'I love you' like always but again, words were not to be had. Mama didn't seem to be able to say anything either, instead she bent over and kissed Martha's forehead again. She felt a hot tear spill onto her forehead as her mother pulled away. She rolled over onto her side, facing the wall and let her tears fall freely. She didn't make a sound or even change her breathing.

Martha's father approached her. He really was handsome. Mama hadn't been exaggerating at all. He walked slowly but steadily. His straight gait, though gradual, was almost regal. He had long legs and as he got closer, she could see his light brown hair was perfectly straight and beautifully styled. It was short, but reached his ears and came down his forehead about halfway then was swept to the side. When he came directly in front of her, he knelt until he was at eye level with her. His eyes truly did look just like hers. He didn't reach out to touch her, but she could tell he wanted to hug her with everything that he was. "I have always loved you, my perfect daughter, Martha."

Her eyes opened suddenly, and the love that she had felt so deeply and perfectly a moment before was rapidly diminishing. She looked around expecting to see him, her father. He seemed so real. Too real. Her room was dark, and the curtain was drawn. She sat up quietly still looking around to find him though by now she knew he wasn't there. Her eyes landed on her mother who was fast asleep. Mother's breathing was steady and soft. Martha stayed sitting and stared into the dark of night listening to her mother's breathing for a few minutes before she lay back down and stared at the shadowed ceiling. She didn't know what time it was and though she tried to fall back to sleep, it evaded her. She closed her eyes and tried to remember her dream. Her father's face came rushing back, not as a dream but a memory of a dream. His light brown hair, his beautiful blue eyes, the soft but strong features of his face. His cheekbones were high, and his jawline was defined but not harshly. The way he walked, so tall and confident. No hint of shyness or insecurity, but total love in his voice and in his whole person. If this dream was anything like her real father, no wonder Mama had fallen in love with him. As she lay there recalling each of his features and remembering his every move, his words, "I have always loved you," rang in her mind so clearly. As she thought on those words her heart swelled again remembering the love she not only heard with his words but deeply felt even after she woke from her dream, if only temporarily.

Slumber never came to Martha the rest of that night though she kept her eyes closed and willed to memory every moment she could recall from her dream. If she could never see her father, she would remember this dream forever.

Chapter 3

The sun rose slowly, peeking over the trees on the property until it stared directly through the window of the bedroom. Light permeated through the thin curtain covering the window. Martha couldn't recall the sun ever shining so brightly. She sat up and began getting ready for school before her mother even started waking. Once she was dressed, mama woke and made them both a small breakfast of eggs and toast and some applesauce before sending Martha out the door with her bag and jacket to head off to school. Martha met May and the boys at the edge of the property and they set off for school. The boys ran ahead, and Martha happily stayed behind to walk slowly with May so they could talk without being overheard. She told May everything that Mama had said the day before.

"Wow!" May whispered, her face looking distant in deep thought. "I knew your mother had been married before she came here, but all my mom would ever tell me was that your mother left a horrible situation to keep you safe, 'and here they are, safe.'" Her voice took on a high-pitched tone when imitating her mother. "I had no idea all of that."

"Yes," Martha replied. "I don't know all the details but when I saw Mama's face, I don't think I wanted to know. Besides, when I started asking more questions about my father, she just got sadder and sadder. I know she still loves him, and I can't imagine how hard all of this is for her."

"So, what happened after that?" May inquired, clearly intrigued and wanting to know more. She seemed certain there was more to the story.

"Nothing really," Martha said as they continued to walk on the road towards the school, it was colder than it had been at all this fall yet but neither girl seemed to notice, "I didn't ask or say anything after that."

"Nothing at all?" May sounded dumbfounded. "I wouldn't be able to stop asking questions."

"I think it would have hurt Mama too deeply." Martha replied. "She really looked shaken when I'd said his name. I don't think I could hurt her like that."

"So, you really said nothing?" May asked.

"Nothing at all! We were both quiet the rest of the night." Martha said.

Both girls fell into a quiet rhythm as they walked.

"Are you alright?" May asked at length.

"I don't know." Martha admitted. "I have some answers now, but they're to questions I didn't know I had. I always assumed I had a father; I never gave it much thought until yesterday when Suzie had said all those mean things. But now," Marth paused and stopped walking. May kept walking a few steps before she realized Martha had stopped. May halted abruptly when she finally noticed and turned to look at Martha without approaching.

"But now?" May prompted.

"But now," Martha breathed deeply, "Now I don't know. When Mrs. Anderson brought us dinner, I felt like I could be ok, not knowing more. Not asking anything else. Mama had answered my questions and while it made me think of a whole bunch of other questions, I thought I would be ok not asking them. But all through dinner and the rest of the night before bed it felt like there was this giant some-thing that had come between Mama and me. Like I had made a mistake in asking any questions about my father at all. I felt like I had done something wrong. I kept waiting for

Mama to say something but the only thing she said to me all night was to get ready for bed while she got dinner cleaned up."

"No," May said walking closer to Martha again, "You didn't make a mistake. You're allowed to wonder where you came from. You're allowed to ask questions about your father." May put her arm around Martha once she was standing close enough and when Martha just looked at the ground, May wrapped both arms around her friend in a tight hug. "You didn't do anything wrong."

Martha's heart felt as though it was going to stop beating. Her chest got tight, and her throat began to ache. At that moment, she remembered the words her dream father had said to her, "I have always loved you." And her eyes burned, and hot tears streamed without resistance, unlike the night before, these tears did not come quietly.

"What's wrong, Mary?" May's gentle voice pulled her from the memory of her dream, but the tears came harder now. May moved and held Martha at arm's length and stared her in the eye. "What happened?" Concern etched across May's face.

"I saw him. I saw my father. I saw him in my dream last night." Martha gasped through her tears. "I cried myself to sleep and I don't even know why. When I finally fell asleep, I saw him. He said he loved me, and he looked like the most amazing man. I could feel that he loved me. What if Mama is wrong? What if my father isn't the same person she remembers? What if he is still alive and waiting for her? For me? What if…"

"Martha." May said loudly interrupting Martha's rambling, rising panic. "Martha Rose!"

May shook her shoulders firmly until Martha looked up at her. May had used her real name, a name Martha now knew wasn't used most of the time in an attempt at keeping her from her father, to keep her 'safe'. Her father would have known her grandmother's name. He would have recognized the name Martha Hart as familiar and suspected her of being his daughter. That's why she was called 'Jones'. Why she was "Mary".

May was talking still but she couldn't understand anything she was saying. She turned and ran in the opposite direction back to her small house. Martha could vaguely make out May shouting after her, but she kept running. Harder and faster. Her feet hurt as they thumped solidly on the rocky road, but she didn't care. She ran as fast as she could until she saw the small house on the large property. She slowed only a moment then ran even faster than before. She flung the front door open.

"Mama?" Martha said loud and clear. If Mama were here, she would respond immediately out of concern, she should be at school by now. But no answer came. Good! Mama was already at the big house, cleaning. She would be gone for hours. She went to the bedroom and retrieved her mother's wooden box that she kept tucked under her bed. Martha had discovered this box accidentally when she was five years. She had been playing hide and seek with May. Martha had hidden under her mother's bed and when she found the beautifully crafted box, she had opened it and saw a lot of papers in it. Mama found her shortly after that and scolded her, saying, "These papers are very important, and you mustn't ever play with them." Mama had hastily taken the papers from Martha and put them carefully, almost reverently, back in the box. Though Martha hadn't been able to read yet she could tell they were important by the way they looked and how heavy they had felt in her tiny hands. She hadn't thought of the box at all since. She wasn't sure what brought the box to her mind, but now, her heart sank when she saw the lock that now inhibited her opening it. The sinking feeling only lasted a moment though. She ran to the front door, which was still open, stood on the small porch and looked around briefly before finding what she was looking for; a heavy rock that lay in the flower bed. She picked it up and held it in her hand testing its weight. This would do, she turned to go back into the house just as May came running breathlessly up the lawn towards her. She walked into the house, closing the door and walked back to the bedroom.

Martha put the rock down on her bed, then hefted the box to the bed as well. She picked the heavy rock up once more just as she heard the front door open, her heart stopped briefly when she heard the door close, was it Mama or May?

"Mary?" the concerned voice of May rang from the front room.

Martha didn't respond. She stared at the lock, then at the rock in her hand. She didn't know if she could break the lock, but she was going to try. She raised the stone in her hand and brought it down hard and fast hitting the lock as hard as she could, she felt a dull ache in her hand but didn't pay any attention to it, just raised the rock again and brought it down hard.

"Mary!" May said as she entered the bedroom. Martha didn't look up, she raised and smashed down the rock hard and fast three more times. Martha went to bring her hand down one more time, this would do it, but her hand stopped. She turned her head to see May standing behind her now, holding her wrist firmly with both of her hands. "Martha, stop it. What are you doing?" May asked, concerned and… was that fear in her eyes?

"Mama is hiding something in here. I know it!" Martha said, yanking her arm free.

"How?" May asked, stepping back and sitting on the edge of Mama's bed, "How do you know that?"

"She caught me looking at this box when I was little. It didn't have a lock on it then. Why would she have put a lock on it if she wasn't keeping something from me? This way, I might get the answers I need without having to hurt Mama by asking her." Martha raised the rock again, ready to smash the lock to pieces. It was already bent awkwardly, and she was certain it wouldn't open ever again unless it was forced now.

"WAIT!" May said, standing. Martha turned abruptly; the stone raised high. May startled back, sitting again. She seemed afraid that Martha would throw the stone at her. Martha lowered the stone. Heart sinking. Was May going to stop her from doing this? She would never hurt her friend, and she hoped she knew that.

"What?" Martha hoped she sounded less angry than she felt.

"Your hand," May said, standing again, "your hand is swollen." May gently took Martha's hand that was still clutching the rock.

Martha looked down and saw that indeed, her hand was swollen. It was also bruising. The dull ache she felt must have been her hand hitting the box the first time she hit the lock with the stone.

"I'll be fine, May." Martha insisted. "I have to do this!" She hoped her friend would understand. If she didn't, then May would probably run to the house and tell her mother what she was doing, then Mama would come and stop her.

She would be so angry. If May ran to tell, Martha would smash the lock open fast then take whatever papers she could shove in her bag and run. Instead of leaving the room though, May let go of Martha's hand, sat back down on the bed and nodded.

Martha smiled at her friend in gratitude for her understanding, and brought the stone up high again, aimed then brought it down as hard as she could.

A sharp and painful sensation ran from Martha's hand up to her shoulder. She released the rock immediately and looked at her hand. May stood when the stone hit the floor and took Martha's hand in her own.

"This is bad, Mary. I should go get our mothers." Martha looked down at her hand, a long cut ran from her pinky to her wrist. Blood was dripping down her arm; she opened a drawer and pulled out the first thing she touched. A white shirt. She wiped up the blood then held the shirt to her hand so no blood would drip on the bed or floor. Her hand hurt badly, and she knew May was right. They should have their mothers both come but, then she glanced at the box, and the pain left her.

It was open. The lock hadn't broken after all of that, but the screws that held the latch in place had been torn from the wood on her last attempt at breaking the lock with the rock. It was one of the screws that had cut into her hand, but she had done it.

"It's fine." Martha insisted. "My hand doesn't even hurt that badly. It's just a scratch. And look!" She nodded at the box. "Will you lift the lid?"

May hesitated for a moment, then slowly opened the box for her. Martha looked inside, there were lots of papers, just as she had remembered.

"Pull some out so I can see them?" Martha asked. May pulled out a few papers and put them face up on the bed, spread out so Martha could see them. "Hang on." Martha said as she left the room. May followed.

They went into the kitchen, and with direction from Martha, May retrieved a small first aid kit that May's mother insisted they keep at the ready. May's parents worked at the hospital, so they knew firsthand how important it was to stay prepared for an accident. As Martha pulled the bloodied shirt away from her hand the bleeding continued, but it was slower now.

"This is bad, Mary," May repeated her concern from before, "I think we need my mom."

"It's fine!" Martha insisted again, "It hardly hurts at all." She wasn't even lying now. It really didn't hurt much anymore. The bleeding had slowed already. "We've seen your mama clean and bandage enough we can do this. Besides, they'll both be angry that we aren't at school."

At the mention of her mother's possible anger, May agreed. She wiped the wound clean and then bandaged it beautifully. The blood wasn't seeping through at all, and Martha could mostly move her hand like normal. They replaced the first aid kit, took the bloodied shirt with them, then went back to the bedroom, Martha tucked the shirt into her bag and then looked at the box.

Among the papers May had previously spread out, one caught Martha's eye; a birth certificate. Name: Martha Rose Hart, Father: William Edward Hart, Mother: Elizabeth Lillian Loudry.

Her name truly was Hart, and William was her father. Martha wasn't sure what to do next. She held the birth certificate in her hands, HER birth certificate. Why had her mother so desperately wanted her not to see this box? What on earth could possibly be worth locking up like this? Martha was always a considerate child, she never just ruined things, and for whatever reason, she had always liked paper. Not to tear it or even color on it, she was fascinated by papers and loved to look at them. The day her mother had caught her looking at the papers in this box, Martha remembered looking at this specific piece, her birth certificate, and was captivated by the pretty scrolling around the edges. The beautifully written letters that swept and curved. At the time, she had no idea what the paper was or what it meant, she couldn't read yet, but she had been transfixed by the beauty of it, like most children would look at a flower's beauty. She hadn't understood why her mother had been upset when she found it. Now she thought she did, but she needed to be sure. There had to be something else in this box that she wasn't supposed to know.

She put her birth certificate down and glanced at the other papers May had spread out, nothing looked important or worth wasting time on. She moved closer to the box and what remained inside. On top were some older papers that, at first glance, didn't seem important at all. She pulled them out and set them on the bed. Under those, however, there were dozens of letters. Initially, Martha thought they were letters addressed to Mama, but on closer inspection she realized that they were all letters written to either James Loudry, Martha's Uncle, or William Hart, her father. Mama had written many letters to both. Sealed and addressed but never sent. She pulled out a handful thumbing through them.

"What are they?" May said. She had been sitting on Mama's bed watching with interest but not wanting to intrude. This was the first time either of them had said anything since May had bandaged Martha's hand.

"They're letters Mama wrote to my father and my uncle. But she never sent them." Martha replied turning one over. There was a date on the back.

Martha turned the rest over and looked through them again, this time from the back. They were all dated. Mama obviously never intended to send them, but she must have desperately missed her brother and her husband writing so many letters to them, knowing they would never see them. Martha stopped when she realized there were two letters dated the month she was born. She pulled those two aside and sat on the other bed next to May. One was for Uncle James, the other for Father. She opened the letter to her uncle.

Dearest James,

I want to say I hope this letter finds you well, but I know it will never find you at all. I miss you dearly and I cannot say with any certainty that I will ever see you again. This may well be the last letter I write to you. It still pains me that I do not know where to find you or how to talk to you. You are the only person that would have helped me those many months ago when I fled from Will and Mama. I died inside wondering where you were and not knowing if you were even ok, but I'm glad you were free from Mama.

James, I told you in my first letter everything that had happened, but I never told you why I left, not the real reason. I found out that I was pregnant, and I was certain with everything that I am, that had I not left, both I and our unborn child would die. I never would have been brave enough to leave for myself, it was all for her.

Yes, for her. She is here now, just a few short days old. She's absolutely perfect, James. She looks just like me and Angie. I named her Martha Rose Hart. Martha after the mother who loved and raised us and Rose after our sweet Angie who I've recently learned beyond any shadow of doubt has been watching over us since she passed. I won't go into all of that, but I have felt her with me, especially as I was bringing sweet Mary into this world. I call her Mary just in case Will ever happened upon us. I do not know how he would react if he ever found us. It scares me to think about it.

I love and miss you dearly, Brother. I hope you are well.

Love always, Lizzy.

Martha set the letter down and opened the one addressed to her father, her tears were brimming in her eyes and she blinked them back to read.

My Love, My William,

I have written to you so many times and have burned most of those letters as they were too painful for me to keep. I have kept a few of them for my own remembrance. Each time I write to you, knowing you will never see it, it breaks my heart open again and again.

Since I left, I have ached inside. My heart has been heavy and longing for your embrace. I firstly want you to know that I forgive you for everything. I hold nothing against you and wish with everything that I am that I knew if you were alright. Secondly, I wish I could convey to you the reasons I left, the reasons I stay away now, the reason I can never return. I cannot know what kind of a person you are now; I had hoped that my condition would have changed your heart months ago, but I was too afraid to even tell you what had happened. I never even wrote in my past letters for fear that the letters would accidentally find you, and then you would find me. But I must tell you everything at this time, because looking at our daughter, now only two weeks old, she is perfect. She has your eyes and when I look at her all I see is you and my sweet sister Angie.

Yes, we have a daughter. The night I left, I had recently discovered I was pregnant and wanted to tell you so badly. You were still grieving the loss of your mother though, and with that grief you had changed so drastically. I was afraid not only for my own safety, but for the life of our child as well.

Once I left, I had to imagine that you had died just to keep myself from wanting to return to you. I kept writing to you though, just as I'm writing to you now, and I can't do it any longer. Looking at our sweet baby, seeing you in her every moment her eyes are open kills me inside. Writing to you makes it worse and I want nothing more than to return to you so that you may see the beauty that we have created. She is so much of both of us. But I cannot return. James is gone and I have no way of contacting him. I have no way to safely see how you are and know if I would even be able to make sure that our baby and I would be safe if we did come home.

But I wanted to tell you. To let you know you were a father. To let you know we were ok. To tell you I love you, one last time. Let you know that you're in my mind and heart always. To finally say goodbye and bury the thought of return forever.

No more letters I know I'll never send. No more wishing things were different, because they can't be. I must fully let you die in my mind to make sure we stay safe. To make sure SHE stays safe. That's all that matters now. Her safety.

Goodbye my love, I would that life had been different.

Forever your wife and grieving widow, Elizabeth.

Chapter 4

Martha's tears came hard and in earnest. May didn't say anything, just sat next to her and let her grieve. After a long time, Martha was able to breathe regularly again, and she stood. She picked up all the papers and put them back in the box. Closed the lid and slid it back under her mother's bed, the broken lock facing the wall. The two girls left the house and walked to school. When they arrived, nearly two hours late, the teacher asked what had happened, but all Martha did was raise her injured hand. The teacher left it at that and motioned the girls to sit.

The next hour passed slowly. Martha looked out the window and watched as birds flew south preparing for winter. She wished she could fly away too. At lunchtime, Martha told May to go be with her other friends. Martha just wanted to be alone for a while. May understood and Martha went outside and sat on a bench as she picked at her lunch without really eating any of it. Other kids were running around and laughing but everything seemed so far away. How had everything become so complicated in such a short time? She supposed it had always been this complicated, Mama had just done a really good job at sheltering her. Maybe this was what growing up really was, just recognizing how complicated everything really was.

Crack, a dried twig snapped behind her. Martha didn't turn; she didn't care who it was.

"So, I was right." A snooty toned Suzie said behind Martha. "Not even May wants to be friends with you now that she knows the truth about you and your mother."

"I'm so sorry, Suzie." That was all Martha could think to say to her bully.

"What?" Suzie snorted. "You're sorry? Why?"

"Because I didn't realize how hard you've had it since your father died." Martha replied as she stared at her own shoes. She had no energy to fight or be picked on today. She didn't know for sure if her own father was dead or not, but it definitely felt like it.

"You're the worst person in the whole world Mary Jones." Suzie said angrily as she walked around the bench to get a better look at her would-be victim.

"I don't know if you're right or wrong, Suzie. But I really am sorry about your father." Martha slid from the center of the small bench to the side, a silent invitation for Suzie to sit if she wanted to. "It's not fair when fathers have to die." A tear slid down Martha's cheek on her last word.

"What?" Suzie said again, slightly less angry this time. "What are you talking about?"

"Suzie, yesterday, you were so mean to me. I never really thought about my father before, it's always just been me and Mama, as long as I can remember, but when you were saying all those horrible things about me and my mama, I wasn't even mad. I just realized that I never had asked her about my father before." Martha felt like she was rambling, but she couldn't stop it. She truly felt sorry for Suzie, now that she had a small feeling of what Suzie must have gone through when her father had died.

"Oh." Suzie said with a hint of deflation. She was visibly upset that she wasn't getting the reaction she had wanted from Martha.

"So," Martha continued, "I went home after school, and I asked Mama about him. About my father."

"You did?" Suzie said, finally sitting next to Martha, now genuinely curios where this story would be going.

"Yes. I did." Martha said, another tear fell. "I asked her about my father, it made her quite upset, but she told me that he had died when she was pregnant with me. They'd had a whirlwind romance, married and had a whole future planned, but he died tragically shortly before I was born." More tears came now, and she didn't care what Suzie thought.

"Oh, wow." Suzie said, all cruelty gone from her voice now. She could tell that Martha's tears were tears of grief.

"I never knew him. All I know is that I have his eyes and will never be able to see him. I gained a father and lost him in one single day, and it hurts more than I can even say." Martha wiped her nose with a napkin. Her tears unrelenting. "So, I just wanted to tell you I'm sorry!"

"Why are you sorry for me?" Suzie said, more curious now. "I've always just been mean to you."

"I know!" Martha said, turning to look at Suzie for the first time since she had approached Matha. "But right now, all I want to do is make someone, anyone, feel as awful as I feel right now. And that's without ever knowing my father. I Can't even imagine how much you must hurt all the time with your father being gone. You loved him, you played with him. He held you. You must have so many memories with him, and all of the sudden, he's gone."

"He's been gone for a long time, I'm fine now." Suzie said defiantly, but she still looked at Martha. "I've gotten over it."

"It's ok, Suzie." Martha said. Tears came harder and started making it difficult to breathe regularly. "I know you're not. You try to be brave for your mother. You try to be brave for your sister. You try to put on a face that shows you're stronger than you feel. But, I know I will never get over this pain. And I know you'll never really get over yours. I understand why you pick on me so much now."

"You do?" Suzie said, a tear welling up in her eye now.

"Yes. And I forgive you. And if you still need to pick on me to help you feel better, I'll be ok." Martha said. She saw a flash of anger behind Suzie's eyes, but it immediately turned to full tears.

Suzie raised her arm, Martha flinched back and closed her eyes, waiting for the blow to come. She should have kept her mouth shut. She shouldn't have said anything. Suzie had never hit her before, but it was only a matter of time. But the blow never came. Instead, she felt an arm encircle her shoulders and then another arm. She opened her eyes. Suzie was hugging her. Suzie was hugging Martha and crying.

"I'm sorry too!" Suzie said. "I'm sorry I've been so mean to you. I'm sorry about your father. I'm sorry you had to find out that way." Suzie pulled away and looked at Martha. "Mary, how can you be so nice to me when all I've ever been to you was horrible?"

"Honestly?" Martha said, "I don't know!"

Both girls broke into a fit of laughter and tears. They sat together until the end of lunch without another word but cried and laughed until the bell rang. Martha sat in class after lunch thinking about what had just happened. Suzie had hugged her one last time before going to class, mumbled "Thank you," and ran off.

Years later, more years than she would be able count, Martha would remember that day. The day she had made a friend out of an enemy and realized that Suzie, at that moment, had healed too. She had truly changed. Suzie was no longer the school bully and never picked on another child. For more than a decade following that hug, Suzie would confide in Martha and thank her for being a truly understanding friend. She would open to Martha and would tell her many things that most never knew.

Chapter 5

Martha sat on the cold cement floor of the basement, her bare feet tucked underneath her. The boxes she had been searching through she knew would stir up old memories, but she hadn't been quite prepared for how much those memories would mean to her. She had found a box with small trinkets, and a glistening piece of metal caught her eye. She saw the shine of a corner of it inside a small box with a glass panel in the front. She freed it from underneath the objects that held it captive and saw it was a war medal. Turning it over in her hands, Martha breathed deeply at the new flood of emotion that ran through her. There were so many boxes in front of her, she could make much faster work of this, but she also enjoyed looking through some of the different pieces of history that made up who Amanda was. It was hard to believe that Amanda could ever truly know how grateful Martha was to her.

Martha placed the war medal back in its box and closed the lid. Pushing it aside, she reached for the next box. Opening it she was met with photos. Not organized at all and just thrown in. She started thumbing through them. Some were recent photos; some were prints of much older photographs. Some of the prints looked as though they were over a hundred years old. This was promising. She was looking for a photograph. She knew it was in here, in this room in one of these boxes. She had expected to be looking for hours and hours before she found it, but hope flared inside her that it might just be this box. One photo she looked at was of a family sitting on a blanket having a picnic and another memory stirred inside her mind. She pictured grown-up Suzie as if it had been yesterday.

The grass was damp, crisp and chilly. The dew seeped cold through Martha's clothes as she sat. She had visited this place once a year for a long time and had just said goodbye to Suzie and watched her walk away, back to her car. Suzie and Martha had been coming here to catch up for two decades now. Once a year, every year. It had been Suzie's idea. She credited Martha for her life changing. Martha had simply allowed her heart to share love in a time of vulnerability with someone else who had been grieving the way she had been. She loved Suzie deeply and hoped Suzie knew how much she cared for her. Suzie had told Martha all about her little baby girl that day. She was just two months old.

"Oh Mary." Suzie had said, "She's absolutely perfect. I'll bring her next time so you can see her. It's getting too cold out and I didn't want her to catch something. She's so little and delicate."

Suzie, who simply went by Sue now, had told Martha during their previous visit, that she was worried she would never have children. Suzie and Jonathan had been married for nearly ten years and still hadn't been able to get pregnant. The doctor hadn't been able to find anything wrong. Sue told her then that she always felt like things worked out when she confided in her.

"Mary," Suzie said, Martha laughed a little that Suzie still called her Mary after all these years, but realized she still called her Suzie instead of Sue, "I wanted you to know, that we named her Mary Sue." Martha's heart filled to the brim with joy and love for her friend. "I don't know if you truly know how much your kindness shaped the trajectory of my life. I know I would not be the person I am today without your kindness and love, my sweet friend. It's amazing how much I've missed you lately." Suzie finished catching Martha up on all the different things that had happened over the last year, then they ended their visit quickly as Suzie needed to get back to the house to take care of little Mary.

Martha stayed sitting on the grass for almost an hour after Suzie had left, pondering over the visit and what it meant to her. A firm hand on her shoulder brought her out of her reminiscing. She hadn't heard anyone approaching she'd been in such deep thought. She looked up and saw those two beautiful blue eyes smiling down at her again.

"It's time." That was all he said, though the broad smile on his face said volumes more.

Martha took his hand, and her father helped her stand, and they walked off together, hand in hand.

Martha placed the photo of the family picnic in the growing pile on the floor. She looked through all the pictures carefully, but none of them was the one she was looking for. Upstairs, she heard Amanda in the kitchen, she sounded like she was getting a snack. Martha smiled, she should be very hungry by now, being pregnant with her second child. Martha heard the fridge open and close, then heard the microwave click open and snap shut. Beep beep beep beep. Humm. The smell of leftover pizza filled the house after Amanda had pulled it out of the microwave. She briefly wondered if Amanda would come downstairs, but then the TV in the front room turned on. Martha turned back to her task.

The next box contained more papers, nothing looked very promising in here. She set that box aside. As she scanned the contents of yet another box, her mind turned again to the day she and Suzie had become friends.

Chapter 6

When school was over, May and the boys met up with Martha at the front of the school and they started the walk home. The six of them were supposed to stay together but the boys always ran ahead. May stayed with Martha to talk, as always.

"I saw you talking to Suzie at lunch, are you ok?" May asked concerned.

"I am!" Martha said, smiling for the first time since yesterday when Suzie had been so mean. Had it only been yesterday? It seemed ages ago. "I think," Martha paused, then began again, "I think we're friends now, actually."

May didn't say anything but she stopped dead in her tracks and stared at Martha as though she had grown a tail.

"What?" Martha asked.

"Friends?" May questioned. "Friends with Suzie?"

Martha nodded and turned to continue walking. A smile spread across her face as she listened to May jog to catch up behind her. Martha wasn't sure if Suzie and she would ever be close, surely not ever as close as she and May were, but they had become friends. The walk home was quiet after that; May was clearly not sure what to say and seemed baffled by the "Suzie is now a friend" revelation. Martha was deep in thought as they walked, the sound of gravel underfoot seemed soothing today. Martha was still grieving for the loss of her father but talking with Suzie had helped somehow. She was still sad but a little more at peace.

As they approached the big house, May stopped, "Mary, are you going to come over to the house today?"

Martha looked at the big house and then towards her own smaller one, shook her head and smiled. "I think I need to talk with Mama and make sure she knows I'm alright, and make sure she's alright too."

The girls waved to each other as they walked to their individual homes.

Martha walked through the front door, "Mama?" she said loudly, the smell of hot cookies meeting her before she asked, "Where are you?"

"In the kitchen." Was the reply. Mama's voice sounded sad but not depressed or worried. That was good.

Martha walked into the kitchen and straight to her mother who was washing dished at the sink. Wrapping her arms tight around Mama's waist, Martha said, "I love you so much!"

"I love you too!" Mama said, drying off her hands, then Martha felt her mother's hands grasp her elbows. Martha's eyes closed tight, relishing her mother's touch before, "What did you do to your hand?"

"Oh," Martha pulled away quickly and Mama turned, looked Martha in the eye and grabbed her arm gently inspecting the bandages. "I hurt it during school." Martha reasoned that she hadn't lied. It had been during school when she hurt herself, she just left out the part that she wasn't at school when it happened.

Mama furrowed her brow turning Martha's hand back and forth in her own. "Are you alright?"

"Yes. It was cleaned and bandaged." Matha insisted.

"Are you sure?" Mama asked, doubt stretched on her face.

"I'm sure." Martha smiled as she gently pulled away from her mother's grasp. The last thing she wanted was to raise suspicions in her mother and add more strain to their relationship. Martha walked to the table and sat down, Mama followed. She had to change the subject from her hand or there would be problems. "Mama," Martha said as her mother pulled out the chair next to her and started reaching for her hand again, "Can we talk about last night?" Mama forgot the intended investigation of the wound and let her hand fall into her lap. There was a moment of anticipation and reluctance which was quickly replaced by determination.

"Of course." It was a curt response, but sincere. "What do you want to talk about?"

"I just wanted to let you know I was ok." Relief flooded Mama's face and Martha took a breath to allow her mother time to process that she wasn't about to ask a million questions about William Hart, her father.

"Are you sure?" Repeating the question she'd asked about Martha's hand.

"Yes. I'm alright." The look on Mother's face proved that she would need more than that to convince her. Martha stood, and walked to the counter, "May I have a cookie?" She asked grabbing one at the same time Mama nodded yes. She took a big bite, smiled and sat back in her seat across from her mother. "Last night," Martha began once she swallowed her bite, "after we had talked, I wasn't ok at all." She took another bite and chewed and swallowed quickly. She hoped that eating would help her assure her mother that she was telling the truth. "I had asked all the questions I had, but by the time I was going to bed, I realized that I had so many new questions. This morning I was angry and hurt, but during school," she was careful to make sure and say during school again, as she had come to these realizations at home, "I was thinking, that if I was this sad and angry about my Father after only knowing about him for a few hours, how sad and hurt you must feel all the time."

A tear escaped Mama's eye, and Mama nodded once. Not a sound escaped her lips.

"So," Martha continued, "I decided that I have all the answers I need, maybe not all the answers I want, but all the answers that I need. And if you ever want to talk about him, I'd be happy to listen." Martha paused to gauge her mother's reaction, she saw trepidation in her mother's countenance, so she continued. "But if you never want to talk about any of it, that's ok too! I know you have been through a lot, and I understand that everything you do and have done is because you love me and want to keep me safe."

Mama stood so abruptly it made Martha jump a little, but as Mama scooped Martha into a huge hug she relaxed into it and wrapped her arms around her mother.

"You are the bravest, most kind and understanding girl in the world, Martha Rose. I love you so much! Thank you for understanding and being patient with me."

Martha's heart sank a little as she heard her mother's words. She wasn't kind or brave. She was lying to her mother by not telling her about the box, about her hand, about the letters or about her true feelings. She wasn't patient at all. She did understand though, and she didn't want her mother to worry any longer. She wanted to make sure that her mother was ok too. It seemed that she would be now. They spent the rest of the evening in their small house, talking and laughing as though nothing had happened. Life was back to normal, or at least it seemed to be for Mama. Martha, however, couldn't stop thinking about the letters. What else had Mama written to Uncle James and her father? The temptation to look through and read all the letters was nearly overwhelming.

When night fell, as Martha lay awake in bed, long after Mama had fallen asleep, her thoughts dwelled solely on the box of secrets hiding under Mama's bed only a few feet away from where she was. Feelings of unrest and anxiety started to creep up on her and held her tightly. She really wasn't ok, she really did need more answers than she had, but she wasn't going to ask her mother this time. There had to be another way to find something out. Hot anger replaced the anxiety, and resentment started to creep in. She was so mad at her mother for keeping all this a secret for so long! Then, anger quickly turned to grief again. Greif of the loss of a father. He really was as good as dead. Even if he was alive, how would she begin to know where he was? Tears pooled on Martha's pillow as she silently cried herself to sleep for the second night in a row.

The sun rose and Martha lay in her bed numb from crying so much for the last two days. Her mother's words seemed far away and hurried. She focused, trying to comprehend the sound.

"I said its time to get up, sleepy!" Mama said as she walked into the bedroom, tossing a clean shirt onto the foot of Martha's bed. "Quickly, you need to get up and out the door or you'll miss being able to walk with May and the boys." Mama grabbed her working sweater out of the closet, and she left the room again.

Martha wanted nothing more than to lay there and sleep all day.

"Hurry quickly, I want to change your bandage before you get off today too." Mama said as she walked past the bedroom door. At that, Martha jumped to her feet and dressed quickly.

As she stumbled into the kitchen with one shoe on, she paused at the doorway, holding onto the molding for support as she pulled the second shoe on. At that moment there was a knock on the door. Martha walked to the door and opened it to find May standing on the porch with her brothers restlessly pacing on the grass behind her.

"You ready to go? We're going to be late again." May whispered as Martha opened the door.

"I know." Martha replied without bothering to keep her voice down, "I'll be right out. Wait for me."

"Ok, but hurry."

"Mama," Martha said as she left the front door open and walked towards the kitchen, Mama had gone back into the bedroom. "I'm going to leave with May, we're running late."

"If you're running late now," Mama yelled from the bedroom, she was clearly busy doing something was keeping her from running to the kitchen, "you'll not be much later if you wait for me to change your bandage."

"I'll have them change it at school, Mama." Martha grabbed a piece of bread and shouted, "Bye! I'll see you after school."

"Martha Rose! Get back here this…" but Mama's protests were cut short as the door slammed behind Martha as she and May ran to catch up to the boys who'd grown impatient and left without the girls.

Martha didn't dare look back at her small house for fear of seeing Mama's furious look at the door. She just kept running until she and May had rounded the corner and were on the road with the trees blocking the view of their homes. They saw the boys just a few paces ahead of them and slowed to match their speed.

"How is your hand?" May broke the silence, "I heard your Mama say she wanted to change the bandage. You should have let her."

"I don't want her to see it, May. She'd probably ask more questions than I want to answer. I don't know how mad she would be if she finds out that I broke into that box." Martha's mind immediately flew to the box, and the birth certificate inside. "Wait!" Martha stopped walking.

"What is it?" May asked, more frustrated than Martha had expected her to be.

"My birth certificate is in that box!" Martha's smile was wide, and she felt as though she would burst with excitement.

"So?" May said, glancing back at the boys, who were getting farther and farther ahead of the girls. She looked back at Martha, even more irritated now.

"So," Martha continued, bouncing now, "It may say where my father was from!"

"Mary," May said, concern in her voice, "we need to go! I can't be late again."

Martha stood still, not sure she was fully understanding the tone in her friend's words. "What?" was the only thing she could think to say to her.

"Mary," May said, gently as she started backing away and moving in the direction of her brothers, "I know this is important to you and I want to help you but if I'm late again, my mother will be so upset, and I'll have to tell her everything. I don't want to get in trouble, and I don't want to get you into trouble either."

"But I…." Martha looked back behind her towards her house, where she knew there was more information, "but what about my father?"

"The box will still be there when we get back. Let's go to school." May was still walking backwards but slowly. "Please, let's do this after school."

Martha stood, staring at her friend, unable to move in any direction. If she waited until after school, her mother would be home waiting for her. If she waited until the weekend, she wouldn't be able to find anything out either, because her mother would be around the whole time. Martha looked at May, not wanting to disappoint her or hurt her friend. Not wanting to get May in trouble either, but unable to let this go. She shook her head and turned slowly around toward the way back home.

"MARTHA! PLEASE! COME WITH ME!" May shouted.

"I can't." Martha turned around and looked at her friend again, May had stopped walking now but looked as though she were crying. She was far enough away that Martha couldn't be certain if she was crying or not. She ran and caught up to May. When she did, she threw her arms around her friend and started crying too, May was sobbing and breathing heavy.

"What do you mean you can't?" May said holding tighter to Martha than she ever had.

"I mean, I have to do this!"

"No, Mary, you don't. It can wait until later."

"May, what if my father is alive? What if he's not what my mother thinks? What if he's changed? What if…"

"What if he hasn't, Martha Rose?" May asked, the use of her middle name stung this time, and she pulled away from her friend.

"What do you mean?"

"I mean, your mother left to protect you. She left everything she knew and loved behind. She came here with nothing, just to save you!"

"But he was in my dream! He looked just like Mama said he did, and he seemed so kind and told me he loved me!"

"It was a DREAM, Martha. Just a dream. Nothing more." May stood defiant in the wake of Martha's stare. "I've had dreams where I was certain I was flying and that wasn't real either."

"This one was." Martha said, determined, taking a step backwards.

"Martha! PLEASE! Listen to me, this could be dangerous." May's eyes were pleading, and her tears came fast and torrential.

"I know he's different now, May." Martha said. She couldn't deny what she felt to be true.

"Martha, you can't possibly know. You don't even know if he's actually alive or dead. You cannot know the kind of person he is now."

May was still using Martha's real name. She must be angry with her. Rather than fight back, she simply said, "I know. But I must find out."

"Martha," May's voice was barely above a whisper now, "I'm worried about you."

"I know. You don't have to come with me, I'll try to come along soon, but I do have to do this." Martha said, giving May one last quick hug before turning back around and heading home.

May didn't hug her back, she just turned and walked a few steps before wiping her eyes and then ran to catch up to her brothers.

Martha ran as fast as she could to the yard and peered carefully around the trees to make sure she didn't see any sign of Mama. Rather than cut across the lawn, she walked around the perimeter of the yard, hugging the trees so she could duck behind them if she caught a glimpse of Mama or anyone else from the big house. She and Mama had shared everything up till this point, she thought anyway, but the revelation about her father, and everything that had happened before she was even born was weighing heavily on her mind. She didn't want to keep secrets from her mother, but Mama had hidden some big secrets of her own for a very long time. She needed answers but also didn't want to hurt her mother anymore with additional questions. If everything ended the way she hoped, her mother would be happy in the end. They could be reunited with her father, all of them, a real family.

The grass was still damp with cold morning dew, and Martha could see her breath in front of her when she exhaled. Fall was approaching fast, and she couldn't help but picture Christmas with her mother and her father this year. As she stepped around the last tree, she crept quietly around to the back of the small house she and her mother shared, and peered into the kitchen window, to make certain no one was there. It seemed empty.

Martha quietly and quickly walked back around to the front of the house and entered the front door. The house was quiet. She wasn't feeling as brave as she had yesterday, May wasn't with her. So instead of calling out to Mama, she was silent. She set her bag down on the armchair Mama liked to read in and walked quickly to the bedroom. She peered under Mama's bed; the box had been untouched. Martha had placed the box with the broken latch facing the wall so that if Mama had looked under the bed, it wouldn't immediately speak to any foul play on Martha's part. Martha sat up straight and looked around the room, she felt she was being watched, but she saw no one there. "Mama?" the quiet timid sound escaped from her lips without permission. There was no answer. She shook off the feeling as best she could and bent down to retrieve the box.

She pulled it out and lifted it onto her own bed, then seeing her bandaged hand, thought she really had better change the bandages. She left the box unopened, on her bed and retrieved the first aid kit and did her best to replace the bandage on her own sitting at the kitchen table. She unwrapped the bandage and looked at her hand in a grimace, it didn't look good. The scratch was deeper than she had initially realized and was bright red even though it wasn't actively bleeding. The skin around it was yellow, but she decided that it was due to the iodine May had used to clean it. She washed her hands as best she could in the sink and then sat down to replace the bandage. She put more iodine on it, and a fresh bandage. Threw the old dressings away, hidden under a lot of scraps already in the garbage bin, replaced the first aid kit and went back to the bedroom.

Martha reached to open the box and hesitated. The feeling of being watched was stronger now, she didn't have to turn to look at the bedroom door, but she did anyway. No one was there. She whipped around and looked out the window, no one was there either. She was being paranoid! She was only thinking she was being watched because she was alone, and she knew that if Mama came home now, she would be furious. For a moment, she thought of putting the box back and running to school, but the moment passed quickly. She lifted the hinged lid of the wooden box, the broken lock looking menacingly back at her. Peering inside, she saw her birth certificate lying on the top of the contents. She lifted it out carefully as if it were the rarest piece of treasure to ever grace the earth; to Martha, it was just that. As she looked at the paper, she realized it was all there. She read it again as if for the first time, this time taking it all in.

North Carolina State Board of Health, Bureau of Vital Statistics, Standard Certificate of Birth. Full name of child: Martha Rose Hart. Sex of child: Female. City: Bath. Twin, triple or Other was blank, as was number in birth order. Parents married? Yes. Date of birth was blurred but she didn't need to see that, she knew her birthday. The next row said, Father, full name: William Edward Hart. Mother Full Maiden Name: Elizabeth Lillian Loudry. Father Residence: Unknown.

Martha's heart stopped. Of course, her mother wouldn't know what to put as his address, or wouldn't want to put it down. Thinking about it now, she may have deliberately not written it so she could claim he'd left her. If she was honestly afraid for their safety that would make sense. She felt tears welling up and a few escaped before she could read more. She stopped looking at her mother's information and only focused on that of her father, William. It was comforting to at least know his name.

Father color or race: White. Age at last birthday: 28. Birthplace: San Francisco CA.

California!? They were all the way from California? She realized that there was no way of knowing if he had stayed in California his whole life or if his family had moved after he was born, there was really no way of knowing. She replaced the birth certificate and put the closed box back in its place under Mama's bed. She gathered her bag from the armchair and ran across the lawn as fast as she could, she couldn't miss the whole day of school.

Martha got to the school just as lunch started and ran to May, excited to tell her all that she had learned. May, it seemed, was less eager to know it. She turned and walked away without a word once she saw Martha.

"I think she's mad at you." Said a voice behind Martha, accompanied by footsteps approaching her. Martha turned to see Suzie, all smiles, "I thought you were sick?" She added with a wink.

"I'm feeling better now." Martha replied, looking back one more time at May who was now sitting on the bench nearest the school. "Wait, sick? Why is she mad?" She looked back at Suzie.

"She told the teacher you weren't feeling well this morning so you wouldn't be here today. When May sat down in her seat, she started blushing badly and then put her head down on her desk and wouldn't talk to anyone all morning." Suzie informed her. "I knew she was lying for you. I assumed it was something to do with your dad."

"Yeah, it was." Martha said, looking around to see who else might be listening to their conversation.

"Are you ok?" asked Suzie. Martha was glad that Suzie wasn't picking on her, and though she'd felt that they were friends, it was still a little unnerving to have Suzie genuinely care about her.

"I think so." Martha said. "Can I trust you?"

The question seemed to hurt Suzie, but she also smiled sincerely and replied, "Mary, I have never once cried with anyone, not even my own mother, until yesterday when I cried with you. I'd never told any of my friends anything about my dad, how I felt or any of it. But you knew, without me having to say anything. I think we are well passed wondering if we can trust each other." Suzie's response touched Martha.

"Can I tell you something?" Martha paused, "I just don't want you to start hating me again."

"I never hated you Mary, I just saw a chance to make myself feel a little better picking on you because I assumed you'd had it worse than me. I really am sorry about that."

"Ok, but you can't tell anyone else." Martha insisted.

"Not even May?" Suzie asked, glancing behind Martha.

"No. Not even May. I'll try to tell her later, but she clearly doesn't want to talk to me now. And I have to tell someone!"

"OK! Let's go sit over there." Suzie said, pointing to the tree where she had been so unkind to her just a few days ago.

They walked together and sat under the large tree. Martha confided in Suzie everything she had learned about her father, catching up on everything she had talked to her mother about. How her mother had told her that her father had died, even though she wasn't sure.

"Now, all you know for sure is that your dad was born in California?" Suzie asked.

"Yes. I feel like I need to know if he's alive or not, but I don't know how to find anything out. I just don't want you to hate me again if my father is alive!" Martha said, feeling more dejected than relieved like she thought she would.

"Hmm." Suzie said. "First, I don't think I could ever go back to not being your friend. Even if your father is alive, you still understand me more than anyone else I know. Secondly, now, don't hate ME, ok? But May is right, and I agree with her."

"About what?"

"About this being potentially dangerous."

"But, what about my dream?"

"It sounds like a dream, Mary. Nothing more than that."

"If anyone else said that I don't think I'd listen." Martha pouted.

"So, because I lost my dad, I'm more reliable?" Suzie sounded offended.

"I didn't mean it like that." Martha said, apologetically. "I just meant that you're the only one that might be able to understand."

"Oh, I do. I have dreams about my dad all the time." Suzie paused, looking thoughtful. "That's another thing I've never told anyone else before."

"You do?"

"Yes. Almost every night."

"Is that weird?" Martha asked. She felt like she wanted nothing more than to see her father, even if it was only in her dreams.

"No. I love being able to see him. It's almost like he's still here some days."

"I wish I could see my dad in my dreams again." Martha said. She could feel tears welling up again.

"Wow." Suzie said, "You cry a lot."

"Sorry." Martha wiped her eyes quickly, trying to gain composure.

"It's ok. I'm glad we're friends enough to talk. I've never had a friend I could really talk to before." Suzie said, wiping her own eyes.

"You haven't?" Martha asked.

"No." Suzie said, and she unexpectedly leaned over and gave Martha another hug. Just then, the bell rang, and they both stood and ran to the school.

Chapter 7

"Suzie again?" May said as she ran to catch up to Martha after school.

"What is that supposed to mean?" Martha asked more defensively than she intended.

"She was always so mean to you! Why are you doing this?" May wouldn't look at Martha, and she looked angrier than Martha had ever seen her.

"I'm not doing anything!" Martha snapped and quickened her pace. If May was going to act like Martha was nothing more than a criminal to be interrogated, then she didn't want to be around her. Martha walked as quickly as she could without running and didn't even glance at May. She could hear May struggling to keep up though, just behind her.

"I'm sorry, Mary." May said eventually, now panting with the effort of keeping up. "I just don't want to see you get hurt. You have been through so much the last week, and I really can't do anything to help you. But I want to! Just tell me what I can do."

Martha stopped dead in her tracks without warning and May bumped into her, nearly knocking her over. Martha's frustration was apparent as she wheeled around at her.

"How about you just try to understand what this feels like, instead of acting like you're better than me."

"I'm not." May mumbled, staring at the dirt road and her feet. The next words were barely a whisper. "Mary, you're my best friend. My only friend. I love you. I don't have anyone else to really talk to but you."

"What are you talking about? You have lots of friends. You're always talking to every person at school."

"Talking to yes, but not about anything that's important. Not anything that matters. When I was upset today, before you came to school, not one person even cared enough about me to notice" May's eyes were tear filled, and Martha could tell she was fighting back against them.

"Suzie did." Martha said as she turned around and resumed her walk back home, slower this time, but still faster than she would normally walk. The boys were already far ahead of them, but she didn't care. She wasn't at all wanting to go home, but didn't have an alternative, especially if May was going to act this way; but she slowed her pace again, this time to a sluggish walk.

"She what?" May asked, Martha didn't respond immediately, she was upset with everything and everyone right now and didn't have the energy to talk to May if she wasn't going to keep up with her, especially with how slow she was walking now.

After a few seconds, Martha heard May run to catch up, and she fell in stride next to Martha. They walked side by side, meandering along the dirt road as other students passed them. After a few minutes, it seemed as though they were the last ones heading this direction from school. They continued on, in silence for a long time, and Martha refused to be the one to break it.

"Suzie did what?" May asked after several more minutes of walking.

Martha let out a long sigh before answering, "Suzie noticed you were upset."

"She did?" May said in disbelief.

"Yes, she did." Martha asserted. "She's not as bad as either of us thought she was. She was just really hurting a lot since her dad died and she didn't know how to handle that, unlike me, I guess, who can't seem to stop crying." These words were bitter and laced with resentment. Hot tears, once again erupted from her eyes. Martha's anger wasn't just directed at May. Martha was angry at everyone. Mama, Suzie and everyone else. She had never felt more alone. She spotted a large stone just off the road nestled between a couple of large trees, she veered off the road and sat down, fully embracing all the emotions that were overwhelming her; anger, grief, hopelessness, isolation, sadness, confusion, uncertainty…

May sat on the rock next to her. They were both quiet for a long two minutes before May broke the silence again, "I really am sorry." She said to Martha as she sat rigid, as though she wasn't sure what else to say or do. The awkwardness between the two of them was a cavern. May sat and stared at the road, Martha kept her face hidden in her hands as she cried and cried.

What felt like hours passed, and the sun was visibly farther in the sky before either girl said anything.

"I just don't know what to do." Said Martha in a hoarse voice, wiping her red and swollen eyes. "I feel so lost."

"Please don't shut me out." May snapped. Apparently, she was angry too.

"I didn't! You shut me out!" Martha shouted.

"I what?" May said, confusion and frustration flooded all over her face.

"Yes. You shut me out. First, this morning when you wouldn't help me and went to school instead."

"I needed to be at school, Martha." May spat her name. "A real friend would understand THAT!"

"I did!" Martha raised her voice another octave. "If that was the only thing, I easily could have let it go. But then, when I got to school you ignored me! AND you also told me that I should stop looking for information about who I am. I should stop doing this because it could be dangerous." She was full on screaming now. More tears came and this time Martha didn't hide her face.

"I said I was sorry." May whispered, shame creeping slowly across her face.

"And the worst part?" Martha gasped between tears, "Suzie agrees with YOU." She turned her whole body away from May and looked back in the direction of the school.

Martha heard a guttural sound from May, was she choking? At this point, Martha didn't know if she cared. She made the sound a couple more times before bursting into a hearty laugh.

"You're mad because your oldest nemesis agrees with your oldest friend?" May laughed again.

"NO!" Martha yelled, even angrier now. She spun around again, directly facing May now. "I'm angry because I feel like every single person I know has either lied to me or told me I was wrong. I'm upset because even Suzie, the one person who I THOUGHT understood what I was going through, just told me I was wrong, and I should listen to you, the OTHER person who I feel betrayed by! I'm sad because my own mother, the only person that knows anything about my father, I can't talk to because I obviously care more about her feelings than she cares about mine. I don't know what to do now, and I don't feel like I can just walk away from all of this. I feel so alone. I want to know if my dad is alive or if he even would want me, but my mother insists he's dangerous. I feel I have to look for him, but I have nowhere TO look. So, I'm also angry that I don't even have a choice in the matter."

May wasn't laughing anymore. She looked at Martha with a sad sort of expression.

"And I don't want you feeling BAD for me. I don't need your pity or anyone else's." Martha said as she climbed down from the rock and headed for home. May could stay on that rock for all she cared, but of course she didn't. Martha heard May climb down and follow her.

"Mary, I'm not pitying you. I guess I just don't understand what you are going through."

"Exactly!" Martha yelled, throwing her arms in the air, she stopped and spun on her heel. "You don't understand! You HAVE your father. He loves you. And your jealousy of me, maybe being friends with someone else, is ridiculous. I could have been jealous of you because of your father my whole life, but I never was. I'm still not!" Martha turned around again and continued walking as she breathed a sigh, then over her shoulder to May said, "It never even crossed my mind as not fair."

"Listen, you're right!" May said as she struggled to keep pace, Martha hadn't realized how fast she was walking but she didn't want to slow down either.

"I know I am." That was all Martha could say. She had said her peace. She didn't want to talk to May anymore. May could feel how she wanted to but she also needed to let Martha feel what she needed to as well.

"You're right, I don't understand, and I wasn't being… a very good friend today." May was panting now. "But…

You… have to… Understand… You're not the... Only one… who's going through stuff." Martha didn't slow down.

"I know that!" Martha shouted without looking back at May.

"No… You don't… or you… might not feel like… you were… so alone." May panted harder.

"What do you even mean?" Martha asked, still bitter but slightly less angry, staring ahead at her path and not wanting to look at May. Their houses were just around the next corner.

"I mean… My dad… he's… not always… there…" May was clearly having a hard time breathing now. Martha slowed but couldn't bring herself to look at May or stop.

"Alright?" Martha asked. "What does that mean?"

"I…….... Mean…. He……" May paused, breathing hard, Martha stopped walking, she could see the big house just come into view, she didn't want to go home yet, but still didn't turn to look at her friend, she was still too upset to give her that satisfaction. May just breathed slower and heavily for a minute before she spoke again.
"Mary………… I…………"

"What. You what, May?" Martha spat, then she heard the crunch of gravel. She turned around to see May crumpled on the dirt road completely unconscious. Panic and guilt immediately rushed through her veins.

Chapter 8

"May? MAY!!!" Martha shouted as she dropped her bag and ran to her friend, she dropped to her hand and knees just as she got closer. She could hear voices on the lawn, maybe it was the boys playing. "Help. HELP!" Martha was crawling on the ground now, trying to scoop May into her arms. "HELP!! HELP!!!! MAY, WAKE UP!" May's face was so pale, and she was clammy. "SOMEONE PLEASE HELP ME! May, please wake up. HELP!" Martha heard footsteps behind her, May's brother, Scott was standing there.

"What happened?" He said, running to the girls on the ground.

"I, I, I don't know." She stammered. "We were walking home and she just… she just collapsed." Martha said, a deeper panic rising and tears streaming down her face.

"Here," Scott said, bending down to pick her up, "Give her to me." Scott was young, but he was tall and solid. May was taller than Martha but still small, so he picked her up easily. "Morgan! Run and get Dad." Morgan, the youngest of May's brothers, had just come around the corner. He took off immediately following Scott's instructions. "Mary," Scott continued, in even and calm tones, "Gather your things and don't forget May's."

Martha grabbed May's bag and a book that had escaped it, then followed May and Scott to the large house. Mama was the first one out the door. Martha hadn't expected her to still be at the large house; she should have been at their small one by now. Scott, May and Martha were halfway across the large lawn by the time Mama met them.

"What happened?" Mama said looking at Martha.

"I don't know!" Martha admitted. "She just collapsed."

"I think she had an asthma attack," Scott interjected, "she's only had a couple this bad, but it's happened before. Where's my dad?"

"He's coming any moment. Do you want me to take her?" Mama said, now speaking to Scott.

"No, I've got her." Scott insisted, though his pace was slowing significantly. He was large for his age, but his strength was a little lacking.

"Are you sure?" Mama noticed Scott struggling too.

"I'm sure." Scott said. He didn't play with the girls much anymore, but he was certainly protective of both of them.

Just then, May's parents both came out of the house and ran at full speed to meet them. The other boys stood on the edge of the lawn next to the house. May's father, the doctor, immediately and without words scooped May from Scott's arms and ran as fast as he safely could to the house. Scott and Martha were both embraced by their respective mothers, fear and caring etched across both their faces.

"Can you tell me what happened?" Aunt Ruth asked, as she released her son and turned to face Martha.

"We... we were walking, and she just collapsed." Martha repeated once more.

"What happened before that?" Aunt Ruth asked, gently, knowingly. She stepped away from Scott and knelt on the ground in front of Martha, taking both of Martha's hands in her own. Both ignored the forgotten bandage wrapped around Martha's hand.

"We… we…" Martha's panic and grief took completely over her. "I don't… I can't…" she shook her head and stared at the ground.

"It's alright!" Aunt Ruth said calmly, her old nurse magic working wonders to calm Martha. "Breathe with me." Aunt Ruth inhaled for a few seconds then exhaled a few seconds and repeated the process a few times. Martha followed suite.

"I… We…"

Aunt Ruth could see the internal war within Martha before Martha even realized it was there. "You didn't make this happen, Mary. You couldn't have known this would happen. You're not to blame. I just need to know so we can help May. Do you understand?" Martha nodded.

"But I.." Martha stammered.

"You will not be held in any responsibility, my sweet girl." Aunt Ruth pulled Martha into a tight yet gentle hug, the kind of hug that only an aunt can give, then released her and held her hands again as before. "What happened, there will be no consequences, I promise. We just need to help May, but we can't if we don't know everything."

"We were fighting." Martha said at length.

"Fighting?" Aunt Ruth asked, still the epitome of calm, it was just a question with zero emotion behind it. Just a request for information.

"Yes." Martha paused only for a moment, she hoped it would look like she was trying to calm herself, but she realized she couldn't say what they were fighting about, not without getting into a lot of trouble and hurting Mama at the same time. "We had gotten into an argument at school, and we were still arguing on the way home."

"Even grownups get into arguments sometimes. What else happened?" Aunt Ruth probed.

"I was angry so I walked faster, and I could tell she was struggling to keep up." Martha said, trying to think of facts to help May without sharing more information than was necessary.

"How do you know she was struggling. What did she sound like?" Aunt Ruth encouraged.

"She stayed behind me, I didn't turn to look at her until I heard her fall, before that, her words were all broken up. She was panting hard." More tears streaked down Martha's face. She had cried more this last week than she had her entire life. How did she still have any tears left?

"Thank you, my sweet Mary." Aunt Ruth said, letting Martha's hands fall to the side in favor of another hug instead. Martha held tight to Aunt Ruth for as long as she could. How could Martha have been so stupid? She had forgotten how many people truly did care about her. She'd gotten so caught up in everything about her unknown past that she'd forgotten how much her Mama, and everyone here, loved her. How much her surrogate Aunt and Uncle truly cared for and gave for her. How much May and her brothers cared. How much May meant to her. How much she needed May. She'd gotten so focused on her own problems that she'd let herself forget about May's asthma and pushed her too hard.

"This is all my fault!" Martha said, the sound of her own voice startled her. She hadn't intended to say it aloud.

"This is NOT your fault." Aunt Ruth insisted. She released Martha from the hug but held her shoulders to keep Martha looking at her in the eye. "Accidents happen and people get into fights. It means we are human, and that we care. We rarely hurt the people we don't really love. Sadly, that's part of being a family."

"But I…" Martha started to say but was glad when she was interrupted by Mama.

"But nothing. You didn't do this and it's not your fault." Mama said, taking Martha into her arms now.

"I love you, Mary, thank you for telling me." Aunt Ruth said, and she turned and ran into the house to help Uncle Daniel with May.

"Is she going to be ok?" Martha whispered to Mama.

"Yes." Mama said, though Martha could hear the uncertainty in her voice.

Chapter 9

A beam of bright sunlight interrupted Martha from her memories as the setting sun peeked through the basement window. She shook her head to clear her mind, allowing herself to be in the present once more. She paused her moving things around in the boxes and listened to the sounds of the house. Martha could hear Amanda struggling to get the crying, sick and exhausted Cayson ready for bed. The front door opened and, "Amanda? I'm home. Do you want me to take over bedtime for Cayson?" Jason, Amanda's husband, had come home earlier than expected and Amanda cried now, too, from upstairs in the nursery. At this moment Martha prayed that God would help the sweet little family be able to sleep well and that their baby would soon feel better. She also prayed for inspiration on where to look next and hoped she would find the picture Amanda had been wanting tonight, before she had to leave. Martha closed another box, that last memory of her hurting May so badly, still so fresh and painful. Even all these years later, she knew it wasn't her fault but there was still pain in the memory. How she missed those days with her dear friend. Nothing was the same after that day though.

She breathed a heavy sigh and reached for another box that looked promising. She opened the lid, and more letters were on top. She shuffled the letters aside and found a pile of photos underneath. She picked up a small pile and gingerly flipped through them as she looked at the old pictures. How time changed so many things. Most of these photos were prints from older photographs. Some were newer but all looked aged. She looked through photograph after photograph, each one stirring new emotions. She had never seen most of these pictures but the faces in them she knew were just as much as her own family as Amanda's. Gratitude flooded her heart and spilled over from her eyes as she pondered again on just how grateful she was for Amanda finding her and bringing her back into the family where she belonged; for allowing her to finally feel like she was a part of the one thing she had longed for so deeply it had consumed her tiny, stubborn fourteen year old self. Near the bottom of the box, Martha at long last, found one picture that stood out from the rest. This was it! This was the photo that she had come here to find; a mother held her arm around her daughter, probably 8 years old at the time. It was the little girl's birthday.

She walked slowly and thoughtfully up the stairs as she heard Amanda crying; she was now being comforted by Jason. Cayson was finally in his crib for the night, hopefully he would sleep through the night for Amanda's sake; she was so tired. The last thing Martha wanted to do was disturb Amanda, so she simply placed the old photograph on top of the small shelf at the top of the basement stairs, leaning against the flower vase. Amanda was sure to see it there. Martha crossed the front room and left the house without a word. She knew Amanda would be grateful; she didn't need to hear the thanks herself. At this moment Amanda needed nothing more than sleep. Tomorrow would be a much brighter day.

As she walked back down the street the way she had come earlier today, the sunset glowed with a beautiful symphony of orange and purple, a celebration for all this coming full circle. Her mind flashed back to the most amazing day of her entire existence.

Chapter 10

Sue's hug meant everything, and Martha watched her as she walked away. They had just finished talking and said goodbyes moments ago, when a firm warm hand touched her shoulder. It didn't startle her, nothing startled her anymore, she turned, and her father stood there, smiling.

"Are you ready?" He said, and she stood, taking his hand, and walked hand in hand with him.

"I can't believe, after all this time, after waiting for so long, someone finally found me."

"I feel the same way." Mama said, her smile widened every moment they walked. Martha couldn't believe how good it felt to be standing with both her mother and her father, together!

"How long ago did it happen for you again?" Martha asked, knowing the answer, but loved hearing her father say it. He knew she remembered, but he also loved saying it.

"About five years ago." he said, a calm sort of reverence coming over him.

"And you?" Martha asked, turning to Mama.

"Only a few days after your father." Her smile spread from ear to ear as she looked from her daughter to her husband.

"How did it feel?" Martha asked, she had never asked this question before. She was excited but realized she didn't know what to expect

"Like there was nothing in the world that meant more." Mama said as she took Martha's other hand, and they walked on together.

They walked for what could have been forever but took no notice of the time. Then, there they were, at the most beautiful building Martha had ever seen. Everyone she knew and loved was standing outside, waiting for her, including Sue! She approached the large group that was waiting for her with Mama by her side. Everyone started clapping and cheering. It was the warmest welcome she'd ever had. Sue ran forward and gave her the biggest hug, and May followed closely behind sandwiching Martha in between her two best friends. They released her, and all three stood for a moment tears filling their eyes. Mama took Martha's hand again and led her forward once more. As they got closer to the front doors of the building, Martha saw Amanda, just inside, waiting. As Martha and Mama left the joyful crowd outside, a small select group entered with her, including her father. Amanda was standing just inside the doors, so calm and peaceful but with such a look of anticipation that Martha knew Amanda was just as excited as she was! Amanda smiled serenely as Martha approached her.

"Thank you so much, for everything." Martha whispered. Amanda didn't respond, but a heartfelt tear rolled down her cheek and she smiled warmly, knowingly.

"Are you ready?" Jason asked. Martha and Amanda were both speechless. They nodded in unison and the group of fifteen walked down the marble stairway together.

Martha's mind couldn't stop jumping back and forth between her memories today. Looking through all those old letters and photos had proved that this was a day of remembrance.

She thought back to the week May had collapsed after their argument. May had had a bad asthma attack, and while Mama assured Martha many times throughout that evening that May would be alright, Martha knew that Mama couldn't be certain. Mama hadn't allowed Martha to wait up any longer to see if May would be alright. She insisted on getting to bed well after dark, pressing on the fact that she would need her rest and that staying awake all night wouldn't help May at all.

The next morning, Mama didn't wake Martha at all. By the time she awoke, the sun was high above the tree line and Mama was nowhere to be found. There was a note on Mama's bed though. Martha picked it up and read it,

Martha, I know you and May are closer than most sisters. I woke up early this morning to see how May was doing. She was not awake, but her father was and told me that she would be alright, but her lungs ached, and her chest had been so sore it was hard for her to eat anything or sleep through the night. She finally fell asleep around four this morning, so of course she needs to stay home and rest. I knew you wouldn't hear of her staying home without you, and I am very much aware that you didn't sleep until close to three this morning either. I came back to check on you just after sunrise, and you were still snoring loudly, so I decided to let you sleep as long as you need to today. Once you're awake and have the energy, change and come up to the big house, cook and I will have some food for you. I love you, my sweet girl. May will be ok. No more worrying over her.

Mama

Excited at the prospect of seeing her best friend and skipping school, Martha threw the note down on the bed again, but the action made her hand throb badly. She nearly forgotten about her own injury, and it seemed Mama had also forgotten about it on account of May's asthma attack. She gathered the first aid kit and took it to the kitchen table again. Removing the bandage, she gasped at the grotesque scene before her eyes. The gash, for now it was clear that it was not only simply a deep cut, was flaming red and yellowish skin had spread even farther from the initial wound. Martha felt horrible about being grateful for May's condition. If not for the incident yesterday, both she and May would have been in trouble with all three parents for being home so late, for the wound on Martha's hand and for not talking to either of their mothers about it. Martha was certain, however, that it couldn't be as bad as it looked and she simply needed to clean it better and bandage it better. She disposed of the soiled bandage and went to the sink and washed her hand thoroughly. Scrubbing her wound as much as she could handle. Tears of pain welled in her eyes, but she refused to let them fall; blinking them back hard, she scrubbed more. An oozy scab washed off and fresh blood sprang to the surface. After she was happy with her efforts, though pain radiated through her arm now, she carefully dried and applied the ointment from the first aid kit and a fresh bandage, double layered this time to absorb and stop the fresh bleeding. Then she cleaned up the old bandages and the small bit of blood that had spattered from the sink and the counter. She was careful to hide all evidence of the scene in the waste bin underneath other garbage that had previously been disposed of.

Once the first aid kit had been returned to its place, she felt confident she would be undiscovered in her omission. Everyone would still be more worried about May than her today, if she could just keep her bandage out of sight, she was certain that her hand would heal before anyone would remember that she had gotten hurt. She pulled one of her sweaters from the closet, the one with the longest sleeves. She always wore this one when she was overly emotional or not feeling well. It was a knit sweater, the only one Mama had ever made her. It was made with very soft yarn and was an unassuming brown. The only problem with it was that it was the first piece of clothing Mama had ever knit at all, and while the sleeves were the same length as each other, they were about six inches too long. It was also the last thing Mama knit. Mama had insisted that Martha didn't have to wear it, but it was so soft and comfortable Martha insisted that she loved it, and she truly did. Though it was obvious she couldn't wear it in public, she loved wearing it when she just needed to snuggle into it for comfort. With May recovering, no one would question her wearing it, and it would certainly cover her hand. She dressed quickly then ran to the house.

The wrap-around-porch was a welcome sight as Martha ran up the steps and through the front door without ceremony. This was her second home even though she hadn't spent any time here at all in the last week. She slowed her pace to a walk as she approached the kitchen. She could hear Cook and Mama talking. As she entered, they were both sitting at the large table sipping their tea. A third cup sat steaming but abandoned. Martha smiled as she entered, a small half-smile. She was half concerned for May, half concerned if Mama would question her about either her sweater choice or her hand. She held the long sleeves, bunched up in her nervous fists, she supposed this was how she always held the sleeves up when not thinking too much but suddenly became very aware of the fabric between her fingers.

"Miss Mary!" Cook said, breaking the silence first. Her beautiful nearly black skin always cheered Martha. Her thick black, curly hair was pulled back into her hat, as it always was, to keep it out of their food. "You're finally awake!"

"Hi, Jo!" Cook was usually referred to as Cook, but Martha, May and the boys called her Jo. Mrs. Josephine Andrson's husband had died only two years after Aunt Ruth and Uncle Daniel had inherited this property from his uncle. As Martha remembered the story, the house and the property around once housed around twenty slaves. The property had always been a prominent one in the area and with the spacious house coupled with the rolling grounds there were many who had to help with the work. There used to be five separate small houses around the grounds, like the one that Martha and Mama now lived in. Three had been torn down over the years and only Mama's and one other remained; the other one had been refurbished into a large storage shed of sorts. Jo's family, for generations, had been slaves here. Uncle Daniel's great grandfather was not the typical slave owner though, in fact, he'd looked forward to the day that his slaves would be able to live free lives. He was a wealthy man, and while on paper, he owned his slaves, he still paid them wages as well as kept their homes on the property in good condition and ensured they always had what they needed. In public he would treat his property the way the general public expected him to treat them though they all knew it was an act. In private, they were valued employees and good friends. Jo's own mother was the last person to live in the house that Martha now occupied and had never left as it was the only home she'd ever known. She died happily there, a free woman, certainly joined by her husband who had passed away fifteen years before she did, also a free man. Jo learned to cook and clean from her mother and while she was born free, after her husband had died unexpectedly, leaving her with four children to care for and didn't know where to look for help, she had come back to this house hoping the new owners would give her work, and they had. Uncle Daniel hired her on the spot, knowing her history and that their families' history was so intertwined. She still lived at her own home raising her four children but worked during the week as the cook and a second cleaning lady here. She preferred to be called Cook when she was in her "Working hours" though no one at the house insisted on it and they even discouraged the children from following suit. Only the adults would call her Cook. The children all called her Jo, or Aunt Jo.

Martha crossed the kitchen in four leaps and fell into Jo's embrace. "How's May?" Martha asked her rather than Mama. She was still worried that Mama would be inquisitive about the sweater and be suspicious of her reasons for wearing it.

"May's going to be just fine, Love." Jo said, planting a motherly kiss on Martha's cheek. "You must have slept poorly to be waking at this late hour. It's past lunch time!" Jo stood then and walked to the counter and began preparing a sandwich for Martha. "Worried so much about May that you needed your cozy comfort sleeves, eh?"

Martha nodded and crumpled the sleeves harder in her fists. "Is May awake?" Martha asked, now looking at Mama.

"Yes, she's awake." Mama said. "But you need to eat something before you see her."

Martha nodded and sat at the far end of the table and waited impatiently for her food. Jo brought it over and Martha said, "Thank you," before she hesitantly started eating her sandwich with her one good hand keeping her bandages hidden in the other sleeve which she clutched even harder now, hoping Mama wouldn't notice she was eating with her non-dominant hand. She ate as quickly as she could without drawing too much attention to herself. She chewed and listened to the conversation between Mama and Jo.

"May is looking much better now, especially after lunch." Mama said to Jo.

"She really is. The poor thing. She's been through a lot in one day." Jo replied.

"Jo," Aunt Ruth said as she entered the kitchen, not noticing Martha, "thank you for the tea, and for being so patient with us last night."

"Cook, not Jo when I'm working, please." Jo insisted.

"Oh please, Jo. You've been here all night; you never went home after you saw what happened to May. You stayed with us all to make sure she was alright. Helping with the boys, the meals and the house right alongside Lizzy. You know you're no more an employee than she is. You and Lizzy are both family here."

"But" Jo started to protest.

"No buts, I'll call you cook tomorrow again, if that's truly how you want this to play out, but right now, I just need you two. My friends, My sisters." Aunt Ruth said. And that seemed to be the end of it. She sat down next to the lonely mug and sipped it, relishing the hot liquid for a moment before she continued. "Daniel is worried, I just…"

"Ahem." Mama and Jo both cleared their throats loudly at the same time and nodded towards the far end of the table where Martha sat finishing the last two bites of her sandwich. Aunt Ruth turned and looked at Martha.

"Oh, Mary! You're finally awake." Aunt Ruth said, flushing a little, "Run up and go talk with May. She's awake and has been asking about you! She could really use you right now." Aunt Ruth quickly brushed her eye, was she wiping a tear? "Go on, drink your milk quickly then head upstairs." She urged when she noticed Martha's inquisitive look and hesitation.

Martha did as she was told, though the three women at the table didn't say another word while she did. Martha stood up and attempted to clear the plate and glass when Jo protested and insisted on doing it herself, then shooed Martha out of the kitchen and stood in the doorway watching Martha until Martha had reached the second stair on the staircase.

Once Jo had turned and gone back into the kitchen, Martha climbed a few more stairs very slowly, until she could hear the ladies in the kitchen start talking again, though this time it was in whispers and Martha couldn't make anything out at all. She crept back down the stairs and stayed out of sight, then hid next to the doorway of the kitchen, up against the wall behind a decorative table with a large vase of flowers on it while listening. Mama, Jo and Aunt Ruth were all talking in such hushed voices that she could barely tell when one person stopped talking and the next started and had no idea wo was saying what.

"He's really that concerned?"

"Yes. As a doctor he's seen this before and doesn't want to leave here without him, just in case."

"Her heart is being affected, how badly?"

"He doesn't know just yet, but listening to it, he can tell its strained severely."

"She just pushed herself too hard yesterday."

"I guess so."

"She's had asthma her whole life, anytime she gets overly upset, she'll have an attack, if she tries to run too far too fast, she'll have an attack."

"And yesterday was just too much of everything."

"It looks like it."

"Did May say what she and Mary were arguing about?"

Martha's heart nearly stopped at this question. She hadn't even thought about what May might tell her parents. Was she mad at her? Did she blame her? If she did, May could have told them everything! She willed her ears to listen harder and to not miss anything.

"She didn't say specifically. But I gathered it was because Mary had made a new friend at school and May was worried about being replaced."

"Everything seems so important and final when you're young."

"It really does."

"I remember almost punching my best friend in the face once, because she had eaten my lunch accidentally and rather than being able to talk about and understand anything we were both so defensive that it escalated very quickly." Aunt Ruth said. They all laughed out loud at the thought of gentle Ruth being capable of any kind of violence.

They weren't bothering to whisper now, which meant anything worth hearing had already been said, so Martha crept out from her hiding place and snuck upstairs.

May's bedroom door was open, so Martha peered into the brightly lit room. The two large windows had the drapes drawn all the way open and beautiful warm sunlight streamed in. There was a subtle movement to the air and

Martha realized the windows themselves were also open, inviting fresh air inside and the breeze complied with grace. May was sitting up in her bed, leaning up against a few pillows, reading a book. She looked wonderful. She didn't seem too ill at all. Just then, May took a deep breath which was quickly followed by a horrible raspy cough. Maybe Martha should be blamed for all of this.

"Mary!" May said, once her coughing subsided. She was all smiles now. "I'm so glad you came!" Her voice sounded slightly hoarse. "Mom and Dad wouldn't let me leave my bed. They told me I had to stay here for the whole day." Her words were immediately followed by another cough!

"Are you alright?" Martha asked, concern growing.

"I'm fine," May wheezed as she suppressed yet another cough. "This always happens after a bad attack."

Martha didn't have it in her to tell May anything she'd heard downstairs. May patted the large bed next to her, indicating she wanted Martha to come sit next to her. Martha followed the direction, left the space by the door, walked slowly, guiltily across the room and climbed onto the large bed and sat next to her friend. She was wringing the sleeve ends in her fists again, this time subconsciously.

"Why are you wearing your sick sweater?" May asked looking at Martha's fidgeting hidden hands.

"I don't know." She lied; she wasn't sure she wanted to let May know about wanting to hide her bandage from Mama. "I guess I was worried about you."

"Worried about me?" May asked before she started coughing again.

Martha looked May in the eye and raised her brow. "Truly?"

"It's not that bad." May said, wrapping her arms around herself as she winced slightly in pain. "My whole chest just aches from the coughing last night, and my throat is raw too. I think that is the biggest reason I'm still coughing now."

"Do you need me to leave?"

"No!" May protested in a whisper. Her eyes plead much louder than her voice. "I've been bored to tears since the boys still had to go to school."

"I think you might enjoy this." A deep voice said from the doorway. The girls both looked to see May's father, Daniel, walking into the room with a tray that held two large, steaming mugs and some cheese. He walked to the bed and placed it between the two girls. "The tea has honey and lemon in it; it should help with the sore throat and the cheese will give you some energy without irritating your throat like toast or bread might right now." He bent low in front of Martha and kissed May on the forehead. "Drink up! Doctor's orders." Then he turned and left the room.

May picked up her mug, smelling the tea and then sipped it. Martha followed her example. It was excellent. Likely, the same tea Mama and the other ladies were drinking downstairs.

After drinking a little of her tea, Martha replaced her cup on the tray. May didn't put her cup down but held it in her hands as though she were cold and enjoyed the warmth.

"That really helps." May said, slightly less hoarse. "I'm sorry if I scared you yesterday."

"I'm sorry I was so mad that I walked too fast!" Martha said, unexpected emotions threatening to bring tears. She placed her cup back on the tray next to May's.

"It wasn't your fault." May said, pausing to take another sip of her tea. "We were both upset."

"Is there anything I can do for you?" Martha said awkwardly, not certain what to say next. May shook her head, but Martha couldn't find words to fill the growing quiet. She wanted to ask about what she had told her mother. What she had said about her hand if anything.

"Your sweater... It's because of your hand, not me, isn't it." It wasn't a question. May was looking at Martha's hands again. Martha realized she'd started strangling her sleeve ends. Martha just nodded and looked down and the tea tray, then consciously rested her covered hands on the bed next to her. She felt ashamed for not feeling worse about her friend and thinking more about her own problems.

"I didn't say anything." May said nonchalantly. She picked up her cup again, sipped her tea and waited for a beat before she said more. "I didn't say anything about your father or your hand." She nodded toward Martha at the last word.

"You didn't?" Martha asked, feeling stunned.

"No!" May assured.

"Why?" Martha was so confused. She was so certain that May had been mad enough at her to tell Mama and Aunt Ruth everything.

"I couldn't. It wasn't my story to tell." May said simply.

"But you were so mad at me!"

"I was."

"It was my fault you had that asthma attack!" Martha continued.

"No, it wasn't. It just happened." May said, calmer than Martha could comprehend.

"You could have told them everything!" Martha said feeling emotions rising behind her eyes.

"I could have." May said, nodding, Martha could tell that the thought had definitely crossed her mind.

"You should have!" Martha whispered attempting to keep the tears at bay.

"I can if you WANT me to." May offered.

"NO!" Martha shouted unintentionally, startling them both.

There was a moment of silence then they heard foot-steps approaching the bedroom, and they both turned to see May's father standing in the door frame. "Everything ok?" he asked, slightly concerned. May nodded without a word. As soon as he stepped out of view both girls started laughing until May coughed uncontrollably. Once the coughing sub-sided, May sipped her tea and Martha resumed sipping hers as well.

"I was thinking," May said at length, "I'm glad that Suzie and you are friends now." She sipped her tea again.

"Really?" Martha asked, she knew what she had heard downstairs. "You seemed jealous yesterday."

"I was." May said, sipping her tea again. When she lowered her cup, Martha noticed it was empty but said nothing.

"What changed?" Martha asked, she didn't want to and could never intentionally hurt May. "I don't have to be her friend if you don't want me to."

"I don't want you to not be her friend because of me." May said, sipping at her empty cup. Martha wondered if she was sipping the empty cup because she was trying to not be emotional too.

"Are you sure? You're more important to me than Suzie is or ever could be." Martha insisted.

"I'm sure." May said as she brought her empty cup back up to her lips. Martha raised another eyebrow at May, then took the cup gently from her tipping it upside down.

"I don't think you're really ok with it." Martha said, placing the empty cup back on the tray, and looking up just in time to see May wiping a tear away. She pretended not to notice.

"I am." May insisted. "Maybe not." She countered. "But I Can't make you not make other friends."

"What's wrong?" Martha asked. "What's really going on?" If anything that she heard downstairs from the kitchen was true, she thought she knew.

"I'm just afraid I'll lose you." May admitted, a few tears falling before she could wipe them from her eyes.

"You'll never lose me." Martha said, crawling across and moving the tea tray to the foot of the large bed, then sat closer to May, and grabbed her hand. She wanted to hug her but wasn't sure if making her lean forward would aggravate her already sore ribs. "I can have two friends."

"Really?" May asked, disbelieving.

"Really." Martha said, squeezing May's hand.

"Go close the door." May said after a few moments.

Martha obeyed and when she returned, she replaced the tea tray to its original position on the bed and returned to her previous spot as well. May had a conspiratorial look on her face.

"I have an idea on how to find out about your father." May said the moment Martha sat down.

"You what?" Martha said taken aback.

Chapter 11

The next day, May was still too sore to move much, so all the adults decided it would be best to keep her home from school the rest of the week and reluctantly agreed to let Martha stay home with her in order to keep May's mind occupied as well as her spirits up, or she may not rest as much or as well as she needed to. The girls weren't upset with the arrangement.

May continued to wear her sweater with the extra-long sleeves each day, changing her own bandage each morning as soon as Mama left for the big house. She started getting a little concerned when she washed it well, got new bandages, and fresh ointment, but the skin didn't seem to really be getting better. May didn't ask about it at all, and it seemed May's incident was enough to make everyone else forget that Martha's injury ever happened too, especially since no one but the two girls had ever seen it in the first place.

Saturday, when Mama left, Martha took off the bandage to find that the wound looked somewhat less red and the yellow hadn't spread. In fact, the scab seemed to be doing well! She redressed it and went on with her day.

It was a cold morning, fall leaves were everywhere and she could see her breath when she went outside. She stepped onto her small porch and closed the door behind her but then thought better. She went back inside. Her sweater needed to be washed, she couldn't handle wearing it any longer. So, she threw it in the dirty bin and opted for a different sweater today and grabbed her woolen gloves instead. Everyone was so concerned about May walking around freely, watching her to see if she would have another attack, that they didn't seem to notice the gloves.

Sunday, after Mama had left to go up to the big house and help Jo with breakfast, Martha grabbed the first aid kit once again, but all the bandages were gone. She tore off the last bandage she had put on yesterday that she had worn under the gloves, was relieved to see that the wound looked a little better. She may be able to get away without a bandage at all today. The scab was long a dreadful, but if she was careful to keep her palm to her leg or close to her body, no one would see it. She replaced the first aid kit and settled for washing her hands thoroughly. No one noticed or said anything all day, not even May.

By Monday, May was feeling nearly herself. The girls decided to leave a little earlier than normal to allow extra time to walk to the school without May feeling like she needed to exert herself. They got to the school early and to both their delight, Suzie was there already too.

"Suzie!" May exclaimed as they walked into the classroom. It was time to put May's plan into action.

"Yes?" Suzie said slowly, clearly suspicious of the attention from May.

"You have family out in California, right?" May asked, Martha was standing behind May, happy to let her do all the talking. This was her plan, after all.

"Yes…" Suzie said even slower. Uncertainties were rising. "Why?"

May started jumping up and down and laughing hysterically. "I knew it!!!" May said between laughs. Martha pulled her aside and helped her sit down.

"You're going to have another asthma attack if you don't calm down." After Martha had gotten May to sit still, she noticed May wince a little and wrap an arm around her ribcage.

"An asthma attack?" Suzie asked. "Is that where you two were the rest of last week?"

"Yes." Martha confirmed. "I had to stay with her so she would rest and not be restless instead."

"That makes sense." Suzie responded. "Is she ok?" Suzie asked Martha, then remembering May was sitting right there, turned to her, "Are you ok?" May nodded once and smiled, then Suzie looked back at Martha again. "I was a little worried about you."

"Thanks." Martha said. "She's fine now, her dad just said she needs to take it easy."

At that moment, another student walked into the room. It was one of Suzie's old 'friends', they sat at the seat closest to the door trying to avoid eye contact with Suzie.

"We have to be quick, before anyone else comes in." May said in a whisper, leaning close to Suzie. May sat next to Suzie and Martha took the seat directly behind Suzie and leaned in too. "I thought I remembered you had family in California." May said, excitedly.

"How did you know that?" Suzie asked, suspiciously.

"You had mentioned it once, when you brought that seashell to school to show it off. You'd said it was from a cousin or something in California." May said, trying to brush it off.

"How do you even remember that? I don't really remember that. That was two years ago." Suzie said.

"I remember a lot of things," May said, growing frustrated, "but we don't have time for that." May looked around and Suzie and Martha followed her gaze; two more students had walked in already.

"Ok, ok." Suzie said, hurry up then.

"Alright, so," May said in an even lower whisper, "I was thinking, we know Mary's father was from California. We know his name."

"That's pretty much ALL you know." Suzie interrupted.

"Alright," May rolled her eyes, "that's all we know, BUT I was thinking, if you could write a letter to your cousin, you could ask them if they know of a William Hart and if he's well!"

"Do you even know how big California is?" Suzie laughed.

"I know it's a slim chance." Martha chimed in, "and if they don't know anything I'll let it go. But what if they do? What if they know him, or at least know of him?"

Suzie didn't respond immediately, she looked at May first, then back at Martha, who was pleading with her eyes. "Alright." Suzie said, taking a deep breath and letting out so exaggeratedly that it made May wince just thinking about breathing that hard. The desperation in Martha's face must have been what made her agree. "But we can't use your name, and we must be careful. Also, you need to help me write the letter. I'm not doing this alone."

"Deal." Said Martha at the same time May said, "Done!"

Suzie smiled, it seemed all it took to make a friend was a little conspiracy. Martha was happy to see that maybe Suzie and May would be friends too.

"Oh, and we can't let anyone else know we're doing this." Martha added.

"That's obvious." Suzie said in an aggressive tone but her smile that accompanied the words was a stark contrast.

At lunch, the three of them stayed outside, far away from all the other students and made sure no teachers could hear or see what they were doing. It took the entire break and four attempts, but they finally had a letter that would work. It read:

Dear cousin Archy,

I Was wondering if you happened to know of a William Hart. One of my classmates knew of him a while ago. He was an old family friend, but they lost touch after they moved. We were wondering if you could maybe see if you could find out about him and see how he is.

Thank you so much! And if you could send some more seashells, that would be appreciated.

Lots of love,

Suzie.

"Please promise me that you won't get your hopes up though." Suzie said as she folded the letter and placed it in her bag.

"I won't. I promise" Martha said, throwing her arms around Suzie. "Thank you so much!"

"You're welcome," Suzie said, "are you a hugger too?" she added looking at May.

"Yes, I am!" May said, wrapping her arms around Martha and Suzie. Suzie started laughing and the other two joined in.

After school, Martha and May both said their good-byes to Suzie and the three of them shared a knowing smile. The walk home seemed shorter than usual, even when they were taking extra care not to walk too quickly. Marhta and May stayed with the boys on the way, though the boys admittedly were walking slower deliberately for May's benefit. When they arrived home, they all walked straight to the large house. Mama was still there, finishing dinner preparations with Cook. Aunt Ruth had kept her promise and returned to using Jo's job title again. Everyone in the whole house seemed unusually happy today. Martha went upstairs with May to her bedroom. They discussed the possibilities of finding Martha's father, what that would mean and what that could lead to. The excitement was palpable in the room. After discussing the wonderful possibilities, May grew unexpectedly somber.

"Mary," she said, looking concerned, "Suzie is right, you can't get your hopes up though. As wonderful as it could be to find your father, it might not ever happen. And even if it does, he may not have changed at all."

"I know." Martha took a deep steadying breath, she knew she was getting ahead of herself and allowing her hopes to lose sight of reality. "But I just feel so deeply that he's back to the wonderful man My mother fell in love with. I just KNOW we will be together again, as a family. A REAL family."

"I know you hope so, I hope you do too. But what if he isn't found? California is such a big state, and I cannot even begin to think how Suzie's cousin would actually know him." May was always so realistic that it sometimes weighed on Martha.

"It is a long shot, I understand that. I just…" Martha paused, trying to form her thoughts into words. "I've been so upset about all of this, that it feels so good to have some hope, even if it doesn't turn out the way I want it to." Martha said the words deliberately and plainly as though she expected it not to turn out the way she'd hoped. She realized that May and Suzie both had her best interests at heart and wanted to keep her safe and not disappoint her, but deep down, Martha also knew she would be meeting her father sooner than later. She didn't know how she knew it, but she did. They spent the rest of the afternoon playing with May's brothers and enjoying the last bit of sunshine before winter came.

Dinner was served for everyone in the house, and Jo, her work hours over, had even gone home and come back with her four children to join the family for dinner. It was a celebration for May making such a wonderful recovery. Jo and Mama made a large roast beef and roasted vegetables. There were hot fresh rolls with fresh country butter and some homemade jam that Jo had brought as a special treat from her own kitchen. For dessert Mama had made two apple pies, with fourteen people the pies were barely enough. As they sat eating dessert, talking and laughing all the while, no one was paying attention to Martha except for May who was sitting next to her.

Martha bent forward to take a large bite of pie when suddenly her jaw tightened and clamped shut of its own accord before Martha could put the fork in her mouth. She gasped through her nose, panicked a little as she put her fork down carefully so as not to draw attention, but May noticed. May looked at Martha concern growing evident on her face.

Martha looked at May and, ever so slightly, begged with her eyes to not say anything, May subtly nodded but the concern was still evident on her face. Martha's jaw was locked tight, and it felt as though it had been glued shut. Suddenly, pain shot through her jaw and into her back teeth then down into her neck. She couldn't breathe it hurt so badly. Just as she was about to break and slap the table for help, all her muscles relaxed and she was able to open and close her mouth like normal, as though nothing had happened. The muscles in her jaw were a little sore but that was the only thing out of the ordinary.

"What was that?" May leaned over and whispered in Martha's ear.

"I have no idea. That's never happened before" Martha said, she reached for her napkin without thinking and used her right hand, in full view of everyone. May was the only one that noticed. May gasped and Martha quickly dropped her right hand under the table and grabbed the napkin with her left hand instead, trying her best to look nonchalant.

"What's wrong?" Aunt Ruth asked May.

"Hot! The pie is hot. I wasn't expecting it to be hot." May said, a little too enthusiastically.

"Are you alright?" Mama asked.

"Yes, I'm fine. It just… startled me." May replied to Mama while looking daggers at Martha.

After they had all finished with dessert, Jo excused her family and herself, and Mama said it was time to get herself and Martha off to bed as well. They were about to leave the house when May shouted, "WAIT!"

"Yes?" Mama said and Aunt Ruth asked "Goodness, what is it?" at the same time.

"Can I show Mary one thing in my room before you leave?" May asked. When no one answered immediately, she added a sad and babyish, "PLEASE?" at the end.

"Alright," Mama relented, "but make it quick. It's getting late."

Martha and May ran up the stairs as quickly as they could. Once in May's room, Martha walked over to her toys, assuming that's where, whatever it was that May wanted to show her, but was startled when the door was practically slammed behind her.

"What in the world?" Martha spun to see a fiery May storming straight to her. She backed away instinctively until she bumped into the wall and could retreat no further. She had never seen May this angry in all her life! She was trapped and truly afraid of what she might do.

Bracing for an impact, Martha closed her eyes. Violently, she felt May grab her right elbow. She opened her eyes and looked at May who had so much anger, yes, but also fear, in her eyes. May roughly pulled Martha away from the wall then slowly lifted her arm up and looked at the injured hand.

"What is happening?" May whisper yelled at Martha.

"What do you…"

"Don't pretend you don't know what I'm talking about." May hissed. "You used my asthma attack as a way to hide this." May lifted Martha's hand and turned it in such a way that her palm was directly in front of her face. "DIDN'T YOU?"

Martha had no response. Anything she said would make May angrier. She looked at her hand, May was holding it perfectly at eye level. It was ghastly. While the initial wound did look better, the skin immediately around it was bright pink and slightly swollen. Yellow skin followed that perimeter. Martha had reasoned that the wound had closed and was healing well so the red would slowly go away and the yellow would surely fade. But looking at it now, she had to admit that it looked worse than she wanted to believe.

May waited for a response but Martha couldn't make any sense of the thoughts in her head. She couldn't say anything. Martha wanted words to come but they wouldn't. She closed her eyes, squeezing them tight; she couldn't look at her hand anymore. It was making her sick. May dropped Martha's arm and it smacked her leg. Martha backed up against the wall again, and sank to the floor, uncertain what to do.

"You MUST tell your mother. Tonight." May said it as loudly as she dared without everyone downstairs hearing.

"What?" Martha whispered, expecting a blow from May if she responded in any way that contradicted her.

"Tell your mother tonight." May said, calmer now. She walked around to the side of Martha and sat next to her. "You tell your mother tonight or I will tomorrow."

Martha still couldn't think of what to say.

"Promise me!" May insisted. "I'm worried about you."

Martha could only nod in the affirmative. They sat on the floor until Mama called up the stairs, "We need to get you to bed, Mary. Come down quickly." Martha looked at May, panic rising again, filling her chest with dread.

"Here." May said, she reached to the shelf next to her and pulled out a book. She hadn't even looked at it. "Tell your mother I wanted to show you this and wanted you to read it." May shoved the book onto Martha's lap. Martha looked down, it looked new, as though May hadn't read it yet, Peter and Wendy by J. M. Barrie.

"But…" Martha began to protest.

"But nothing." May said, standing from the floor and offering her hand to Martha to help her up. "If you don't take something down with you, both our mother's will ask what we were doing. If you just carry that they'll assume that I wanted to show you the new book I got, and that we talked about it and I wanted to lend it to you."

"I…" Why were words so hard for Martha to find to-night?

"You may not even need to say anything." May said, pulling Martha to her feet. "Let's go."

May led the way downstairs and to the entryway where Mama and Aunt Ruth were chatting as they waited for their daughters' return.

"Bye!" May said as she ushered Martha to her mother's side. She pulled Martha in for a hug and whispered, "Tell her when you get home or I will, I'm serious."

Martha nodded, "I will. Thank you for everything." The girls pulled away and everyone said their goodbyes.

Mama and Martha walked across the grass to their small home while thoughts tumbled around in Martha's head. So many thoughts, worries and concerns. She knew May was right and that she needed to tell Mama but knew that telling her would get Martha into so much trouble. She could inadvertently get May into trouble too. She couldn't do that to May, not with everything else she'd been through lately, especially since it had all been her fault. She worried and worried about it the whole walk home, and into the house. She thought about how to say it. What she could possibly say without incriminating herself or her friends. She could leave out the part about the box, but then she'd have to lie and come up with some other way she had been hurt. She had told her mother something when it had first happened… what had it been? She couldn't remember. If she said something different, Mama would know she was lying, and she'd be in bigger trouble.

Before she knew it, she was in bed with Mama tucking her in and saying goodnight. How had she gotten here? She felt sick to the stomach knowing she needed to say something and not knowing how. It was now or never.

"Mama." Martha said in a soft whisper, half hoping Mama wouldn't hear it.

"Yes, my sweet girl?" Mama asked.

"You know I love you, right?" Martha asked.

"Of course. I love you too!" Mama replied and bent low to kiss her head.

That was it. No other words would come out of Martha's mouth. No sounds. Nothing. She rolled over and stared at the wall, a tight feeling creeping up and into her chest, she couldn't remember when she'd felt this anxious about anything. The tightness spread into her jaw and just like at dessert, it tightened, and she couldn't open her mouth no matter how she tried. Pain quickly followed shooting through her teeth, jaw, and neck. It passed so quicky though, only leaving a dull ache and Martha free to move her mouth at will again. Hot tears leaked onto her pillow. She was honestly scared. She had no idea what was happening but didn't know how or who to ask for help. HELP! She thought as she drifted off to sleep.

There he was, standing beautifully with his blue eyes and warm smile. Her father!

"Hello, Martha." He said, arms opening wide to welcome her into his embrace. She ran to him, and when his arms wrapped around her, she felt nothing but love and peace.

"I'm trying to find you, but I don't know if I can." Martha told him. She wanted to tell him of their plan to send the letter to California and look for him. She wanted to tell him everything that had been happening since she found out about him, but words were still evading her, even now. Instead, she just hugged him as tightly as she could.

He held her tightly for a long time. When he released her from the hug, she wanted to keep him in her arms and to stay in his forever, but she knew he wanted to say something to her. He took her shoulders gently in his big, strong hands, and he knelt in front of her so that his eyes were level with hers.

"I know you are." He said understanding written plainly across his face. "I know you're looking for me. I've been looking for you your whole life! Since before you were born. I love you so much, my sweet Martha. You look just like your mother. Will you do something for me?" He asked.

"What?" Martha inquired as she nodded yes. She would do anything for him.

"Will you tell your mother how sorry I am? Tell her I love her. Tell her I always have and always will. Tell her," He paused and let go of Marthas shoulders long enough to wipe at his blue eyes. Tears were welling up in them. "Tell her that if she'll have me, I'll wait for her forever."

Martha pushed into his embrace again, burying her face into his neck, breathing deep to capture his smell. "Yes, I'll tell her." She said.

He wrapped his arms around her again, holding tight and turned his face into her neck breathing deeply as well. "I love you, Martha."

"I love you too, Daddy." Hot tears hit her neck and her cheeks at the same time.

"I'll see you soon, darling." He said. "Please don't be afraid, and please tell your mother, if you remember."

Too soon, he let her go, and Martha woke up.

Chapter 12

Martha opened her eyes and lay in her bed staring at the ceiling. She didn't recall what happened throughout the night very well. Her whole body had a mild ache to it, especially her neck and jaw. Had she been clenching her teeth all night? How had that not kept her awake? She closed her eyes and wished the dream to come back. Her father had been there. He'd been certain they would see each other soon. But she couldn't remember much else. She wished he could have stayed and been there when she woke. She forced herself to stand and walk around the tiny room, each step felt like a chore and made her neck hurt. She got dressed and walked to the kitchen where Mama was making toast and eggs.

"You're up early." Mama said with a smile.

"Morning." Martha's voice felt scratchy. She kept her hand hidden from Mama's view and sat at the table bleary eyed.

"Breakfast isn't quite ready yet." Mama informed. "Why are you up so early? I usually have to pry you from your bed. Something exciting happening at school?"

"Yes." Martha said, not convincingly, then she remembered that Suzie was supposed to mail that letter yesterday. "YES!" She repeated, much more enthusiastically.

"Well, I am happy to see you're excited." Mama laughed.

Once breakfast was finished, Martha stood to help clean up. Mama protested, "You'd better get going actually, it snowed last night so you'll take longer to get to school." She looked out the window, May and the boys were trudging through the early snowfall that blanketed the ground.

After pulling on her boots and coat, she hesitated and looked at her hand. It was a little less red and the yellowing seemed to be less too, though the center of the scab had peeled slightly and underneath looked almost blackish. Pulling on her gloves before she could change her mind, she walked to the kitchen to tell Mama before May and the boys got to the small house.

"Mama?" Martha said timidly.

"Yes dear?" Mama said as she was pulling on her own coat.

"I love you!" It was all she could say. She was too afraid that Mama would make her stay home and she wouldn't be able to know if Suzie had mailed that letter or not.

"I love you too! Have a wonderful day at school dear." Mama said as she fastened her last button.

There was a knock at the door and May stood waiting for Martha. "Did you talk to your mother?" whispered and glared.

"Yes!" Martha said. She rationalized that she had, in fact talked to her mother. There was no lie.

"Really?" May questioned.

"Yes, I talked to her." Martha said.

"Hello, May. Good morning!" Mama said to May as she entered the room from the kitchen.

"Good morning." May replied. "Did Mary talk to you this morning?"

"Yes." Mama said quickly.

"She did?" May asked with surprise in her voice.

"Yes." Mama said without smiling, looking a little confused. Martha was worried she'd be found out.

"And you aren't worried about her?" May persisted.

"A little worried. She woke earlier than normal but it worked out for the best." Mama said, clearly in a hurry to get over to the big house.

"But Mary is alright?" May questioned.

"I'm sure she will be. She could get some more sleep tonight I think, but she should be right as rain in no time." Mama said with finality, the questioning was over. "I'll see you girls after school, love you both." Mama gave Martha a quick kiss on the top of her head as she walked past them and towards the big house.

"Alright?" Martha asked, hoping May would let it go.

"Alright." May said after scrutinizing Martha for a few moments.

The walk to school was frigid. They walked through the snow, staying as much as they could inside the tracks on the road left by the few vehicles that drove it earlier. Once they got to school almost everyone was already in their seats. The bell rang only a minute after Martha and May took their seats next to Suzie, they had to wait for lunch to find out anything about the letter.

Once the lunch bell rang, the three girls went outside and trudged a path through the snow to their tree on the edge of the school grounds, even with the snow and the cold it was worth it not to be overheard by eavesdroppers.

"Were you able to send that letter?" May asked before Martha could.

Martha realized how much she took May for granted. May was truly invested in this.

"Yes." Suzie said smiling, but her smile faded quickly. "It could take a while for it to get there, though, especially with the snow, and then I have no idea how long it will take for him to respond, if he ever does respond."

After school, Martha tried not to think too much about the letter. Suzie was right; a phrase Martha had heard many more times than she ever would have imagined just two weeks ago. The walk back home seemed longer than usual, the snow was crisp and crunchy with every step. The muffled sound of winter felt ominous. The boys ran ahead as they threw snowballs at one another. Their taunting shouts and laughter fell short in the atmosphere. The cold bit through Martha's coat and she couldn't focus on much, just each step following the other. Occasionally May would say something, but Martha couldn't focus on her at all.

Eventually they came to the bend that led to their homes. Rather than join May and go to the large house as was usual, Martha headed for the smaller cottage. May, again, said something that Martha couldn't, or didn't want to, comprehend. As Martha entered the small home, a strange distant feeling overcame her, accompanied by a sudden sadness she couldn't explain. She took off her coat, gloves and boots and left them lying on the floor next to the armchair. She abandoned her bag somewhere between the front door and the bedroom and then she climbed into bed. She wanted so badly to cry though she wasn't sure why, but the tears never came. She lay nestled under her blanket, her mind racing over everything and nothing all at once. Her mother was right about one thing this morning, she needed to rest. She closed her eyes and eventually drifted off into an uneasy sleep.

There were shapes and shadows. So much turmoil and chaos. Nothing made sense. She felt a strange sense of love and not belonging. She was wandering in a place full of shadows, there was not anything that looked familiar, but a feeling of love compelled her forward. She walked, blindly in a hazy mist, was she moving in a straight line or in circles? She couldn't tell. Walking on, she eventually saw other shadowy figures walking in the mist too, other people, confused like she was. Some walking in the same general direction she was, others the opposite way. She couldn't make out any features of anyone, the mist was too thick. She didn't belong here. Where was here? As she continued on, the mist grew thinner and some of the people closest to her started to seem clearer. There was so much going on. Some people looked happy, others were clearly miserable. Most, like Martha, seemed to just be confused. Some people, the ones who looked the happiest would approach someone else who looked confused and start to talk to them, she tried to listen to their conversations, but she couldn't make out any sounds. The happy person would embrace the confused one, and the confused person would start to look more happy, most of the time.

One man, very near her, looked oddly familiar though she didn't know why. He wasn't moving in any direction and wasn't looking around much either. He stood still and stiff, staring forward toward where the mist seemed to dissipate, and things looked a little brighter from here. Why did he look so familiar? Martha stopped walking when she saw his eyes. She watched him for a moment, his face blank; not confused and not happy. He was waiting for someone. Martha couldn't keep her eyes off of him, though he didn't seem to notice her at all. He just stood, rooted to his spot waiting for… what? Suddenly his face turned from indifference to obvious hatred. He'd seen something, or maybe someone, that he didn't want to see. Martha turned her head and saw a woman, more beautiful than anyone she'd ever seen, walking toward the man. Looking back at the man, his face was no angry, though he didn't move a muscle as the woman approached him. Her smile was radiant and went clear to her beautiful blue eyes. Those eyes… Where had she seen them before? As the woman came closer to the man, his anger and hatred deepened, he still didn't so much as flinch though the malice he clearly held for her didn't seem to deter her in the least. Martha wished more than anything that she could hear what they were saying, she took one step closer, then stopped, knowing she should not hear this conversation. Understanding washed over her. But she took one step back and resumed watching them from a distance. The Man suddenly turned his head in her direction, then glared daggers before he threw his hands up in the air, turned around, and walk back into the thickest part of the mist. As soon as he was out of sight, a wave of grief hit her so completely that she fell to her knees. Tears flooded from her eyes and watered the ground in front of her. Her hands were buried in her lap, and she gasped for breath. She'd never felt heartache like this before, and she didn't understand it at all. What had just happened?

As she struggled with the soul-shattering anguish that was washing over her, she was certain she would be consumed by it, and it was growing deeper. Suddenly, she felt a gentle hand on her shoulder and the most profound peace replaced every ounce of pain. Peace and love. She looked up, it was the woman with blue eyes! She held out a hand and helped Martha to her feet. She was still smiling, though it looked like she had been affected by the man's walking away as much as Martha had been, just not nearly as deeply.

"It's tragic, I know." She said, comfort like Martha had never known radiated from this woman. "But it will all be alright in the end. His choice will make him happy."

"I don't understand." Martha said. "Where am I?" What she really wanted to ask was, how do I know you. She didn't know how, but she knew she did.

"You're not where you're supposed to be. Not yet. He wanted to come help you," She gestured to someone behind Martha and to her right. "But the time hasn't come." Martha turned her head to see who the woman was talking about, but all she could see was a shadowy figure obscured by the rolling mist.

"I still don't understand." Martha said. She had so many questions. She wanted to ask so many things.

"You will soon enough." The woman said, smiling, and taking Martha by her shoulders, pulling her close. "You will soon enough." She repeated. And she kissed her forehead. Martha looked back at the woman, wanting to ask a question but she couldn't decide which one was most important, and she didn't know if she could even shape any of her questions into words at all.

"I…" Martha started, then stopped, but then couldn't restrain the words, "I love you!" and a tear of joy fell down her face. How could she love this person she'd never met before? But she knew she did. She knew she loved her so much.

"I love you too, dearest Martha." The woman said with a wink. "I wish you could stay."

"Me too." Martha said.

"I'm so sorry, love." The woman said, a tear rolling down her face now.

"Sorry for what?" Martha asked.

"This is going to be painful." The woman said as she grabbed Martha's hands and squeezed them tight. "Just know, you're not alone."

Martha opened her eyes as pain shot through her entire body. Every muscle in her neck and back tensed in unbearable agony. She was laying on her back then suddenly the pain increased, and her back and legs arched unnaturally upward. The pain was so much she wanted to scream; she needed to scream! The sound that came out was unearthly. Gargled moans of a scream that was lost in her throat. She couldn't open her mouth, and she couldn't breathe properly. What was happening? Was she going to die? Hot tears fell down the sides of her face as she continued to groan and spasm in her bed. All at once, peace overcame her, and her body began to relax. Her back collapsed back to the mattress and her jaw released. Her airways were clear again and she was alright. As she took deep and panting breaths, she felt a presence in her room and turned her head as much as she could despite her sore muscles, she saw no one but knew the woman in her dream was right, she wasn't alone and that thought was comforting.

She lay in her bed for a long time. An hour? Maybe more, before she even noticed that the sun was still up and shining light through the window. She tried to sit up, she didn't want Mama to worry, though she had noticed Martha hadn't slept well, so maybe Mama assumed she'd come home to sleep. As she pulled her body to a sitting position on her bed, every muscle in her body protested. She wanted to lay back down and go to sleep. Go tell your mother. The thought was so quiet in her head she shook it off. The action of just moving her head that much sent pain shooting through her neck, jaw and head. Go tell your mother, NOW!

The thought was so clear this time that Martha couldn't ignore it. She stood, shaky and weak, but she stood. She hobbled through the house and struggled with her coat and boots. She couldn't be bothered to button up the coat or buckle the boots. But she would be fine walking across the lawn.

She shut the door behind her, and the distance between the two buildings suddenly seemed impossibly far. Go. Now! The thought came to her as clearly as though someone had said it directly to her. She took one step, then another. Each step brought a wave of pain but also became easier to take. She finally made it to the big house, the stairs up to the porch now seemed like climbing a mountain. She was so tired, her muscles pled for a reprieve. She started to bend her knees to allow herself to sit on the bottom stair when, don't you dare quit now. She stood taller and breathed deeply. One stair at a time. Just as she was about to collapse onto the porch, the front door opened, Uncle Daniel came out and caught her just before she hit the wooden planks beneath her feet. Everything went black.

Chapter 13

Sounds seemed far away from her; she could make out voices but couldn't tell where they were coming from. She tried to open her eyes, but she was so tired. Why wouldn't everyone just be quiet so she could sleep?

She heard rushing footsteps and panicked words.

"What happened?"

"I'm not sure, she just collapsed."

"Here, put her on the sofa."

She was bouncing around and her arms felt unusually heavy hanging at her sides. She still couldn't open her eyes. She tried to lift her arm, but it wouldn't obey.

"There, just there. Gently."

"Someone, grab a pillow."

"Is she dead?"

"No, son, go play outside with Deryk."

"I don't want to go outside."

"Can I go outside?"

"Someone, grab me a pillow."

"No, you can't go outside."

"She's breathing, but she's burning up."

"Scott, take your brothers upstairs immediately."

"I never saw a dead body before."

"No one is dead."

"Jo, fetch a cold cloth, quickly. We've got to get her temperature down."

"What's going on? Mary? MARY!?"

"Ruth. Take her out of here."

"Here's the cold cloth."

"What's happened?"

"I don't know, she's burning up."

"I thought she was resting."

"MARY!"

"Doesn't Aunt Lizzy know?"

"No. Go upstairs with your brothers."

"DAD! Check her right hand!"

"May, this is no time to…"

"NO. Check her hand."

There was someone tugging on her coat sleeve, then an audible gasp. She still couldn't open her eyes or move at all. Why was she so cold? Sounds faded and she was oblivious to the world around her.

Chapter 14

The far-off sound of a train whistle alerted Martha to something outside her own existence. The sharp but distant sound of the whistle came again begging for Martha to regain consciousness but the battle for peace vs pain was strong. She inhaled sharply and was assaulted by the smell of antiseptics and urine. Involuntarily, she turned her head sharply to avoid the strong smell of bleach that followed. The movement made her shoulder move suddenly and a sharp pain sprang from the wrist and fingers of her right hand and shot up to her shoulder and neck. Her eyes flew open to a blinding light streaming in from the multiple large windows along the wall, sheer curtains obstructed the view from outside while letting in the painful bright light. Martha lay as still as she could, hoping the pain would diminish, everything else was taken in slowly, her mind was not able to process all the information she was being bombarded with. The white walls reflected the light, and she couldn't comprehend where she might be. A sudden clang of metal on porcelain drew her attention and she turned her head unintentionally to follow it, sharp stabbing pain radiated through her arm and shoulder again, originating in her wrist. Wincing in pain she closed her eyes and breathed deeply; she immediately regretted it. Urine, chemicals and medicine overwhelmed her again, she nearly vomited.

Voices in the next room were heard, soft at first, then louder as they came closer. She slowly opened her eyes and saw a door. A large, heavy looking door. Where was she? The voices came closer; it must have been a very long hallway on the other side. The door started opening and instinctively, Martha closed her eyes. She heard many voices, wheels and clanging out in the hall. Holding as still as possible, she listened as the door closed, and two female voices were talking in hushed tones. They came closer and closer to her. She heard a shuffling of papers and then felt cold fingers touch her left wrist. The contact startled her, and she opened her eyes and her arm twitched away from the unfamiliar woman.

"Oh goodness!" She said to Martha, "I'll go fetch Dr. Abernathy." The other woman didn't say anything, she just looked up at Martha for a moment then looked back at the papers she was holding. It was a medical chart. Was she in the hospital? The second woman put the papers down at the foot of the bed which Martha had just realized she was laying in. Chills coursed through her body as the women, which Marhta now recognized must be nurses, exited the room leaving Martha alone again. She tried looking around without moving her head any more than necessary, she learned already that movement triggered greater pain. Her whole wrist was throbbing, she looked toward where she expected it to be, and saw, instead of her cold hand, a lump of bandages. She couldn't feel much in her fingers. It was so cold even despite being balled up in a fist beneath the lump of cotton gauze. Memories of the day flooded back to her; she had gone to the large house. She must have passed out, and the adults must have found out about her hand and her wound. What had May said? Would they both be in trouble now? Why was she in the hospital? Who was Dr. Abernathy? The name sounded familiar, but she couldn't quite place why.

Voices sounded outside her door again and when it opened, the two nurses that had just come and gone were now standing again beside her bed trailed by Uncle Daniel! His doctor's coat flowing smoothly behind him, she realized that here, in this hospital, he was called Dr. Daniel

Abernathy. That's why she knew the name. Uncle Daniel walked quickly through the door and smiled broadly at Martha.

"Well, sweet Mary," He said walking closer to her, "You gave us all quite a scare." He broke all professionalism and bent and kissed her forehead. He stood straight and placed his right hand on the top of her head, brushing a few loose strands back off her face.

Martha wasn't sure what to say, so she just smiled back, a weak and exhausted, half smile. It had been a very long day.

"How are you feeling?" He asked, genuine concern and love in the question.

"I'm alright." Martha insisted. "Where's Mama?"

"I sent her home for the night." He replied, gently. "She and Ruth needed some rest. They hardly left your side the whole time."

"The whole time?" Martha was confused. There was still daylight left. How could they have needed rest?

"Mary," Uncle Daniel said, moving over and grabbing a stool so he could sit next to her. He gently held her left hand and squeezed softly as he said, "you've been here for two days."

Uncle Daniel and the nurses had said more after that, but Martha couldn't recall anything at all. Two days? How had she lost two whole days? She had just closed her eyes, that's all!

"Mary," Uncle Daniel said, apparently, he had said her name a few times by the look on his face. "I'm going to send for your mother and Aunt Ruth. Will you be alright alone for a little while?"

Mary nodded. Uncertain what other choices she had. Uncle Daniel left quickly with a smile on his face, and one of the nurses pulled out a bedpan from somewhere under the bed and swapped it with a new one. The second nurse, the one that had touched Martha's wrist earlier, was marking things on the chart, soon they both left, and Martha was alone again.

She lay in her bed, partially propped up with pillows, doing her best not to move and looked toward the windows that fully lined the wall. She couldn't see much through the sheer curtains, but the sunlight seemed warm even though she knew it was most likely snowy outside. She could hear the trains in the distance and traffic of people and horses below and the occasional motor car as it passed. The smells of the hospital were filled with so many noises and smells it took Martha a moment to realize that the smell of urine was now missing from the barrage of insulting odors; for this, she was grateful. She was completely unaware of how much time was passing. Her mind kept turning the events she could remember over and over. She had blacked out, she had hurt her hand a few days ago, she had injured it breaking the lock. She had become friends with Suzie. Suzie and May had become friends too. There had been a reason she had opened that box, what was it? Her father! She was looking for her father. She relaxed a little at the thought of her father. What day was it? Was May at school with Suzie? Had Suzie heard anything at all from her cousin? Had he even received the letter? Had May told Mama about the box, the birth certificate? So many thoughts running through her mind she couldn't breathe properly.

She closed her eyes again, wishing the light would dissipate and her consciousness would fade again. She'd already lost two days and had no recollection of anything of that time, if she could just go back to oblivion until Suzie had a reply, she felt all her troubles would be gone. After a long while, she finally drifted off to sleep.

She was in a bright room, but it wasn't harshly lit. A warm light surrounded everything. The walls were solid, but she was unable to focus on them. She was at peace here. There was nowhere else she would rather be. She walked and sat on a beautiful sofa, it was softer than anything she'd ever sat on before, including her bed. The fabric was purple and had a velvety feel to it. As she admired the fabric her eyes wandered to the wood that made the frame of the seat. It looked as though it was hand carved and had strange flowers embellished throughout the woodwork, flowers she's never seen or heard of.

"Martha." A soft voice beckoned to her. She turned, and approaching behind her was her father again. Love and hope filled her to overflowing and she couldn't stand for fear he would disappear.

"Father?" His paced quickened at her question.

"My Martha!" He said again, more joyful and energized this time.

He reached her and she stood, they embraced for a long time before he released her, but held her hand, and sat on the sofa, she sat next to him.

"I don't want to lose you again." Martha said with tears filling her eyes, her father reached up and wiped them away.

"You never lost me, my sweet girl, I lost you." His voice was tender but full of regret and longing.

"What do you mean?" She asked, none of this made any sense. She was in the hospital. She knew she was still there, but this all felt so real at the same time.

"You never lost me; it was my mistakes and choices that lost you and your mother." It was his turn to have a tear fall, but Martha couldn't bring herself to wipe it away for him.

"No, you're right, I didn't lose you, did I?" Martha said. She hadn't lost him; she never had him in the first place. Her mother had taken her away before she could know him.

"Don't think that my girl." He said as though he knew what she was thinking.

"Don't think what?" She asked though she thought she already knew.

"Don't blame your mother. The only one that deserves any of the blame is me." He said, more tears falling down his face now. "I know she told you some things, but not all, and I won't be the one to burden you with the story, but, Martha, sweet Martha," he leaned forward and held her to his strong chest, "it truly was entirely my fault. I did horrible things and your mother, the strongest woman I know, did everything she could and kept you safe. And she did the right thing."

"So," Martha paused, trying to make sense of what he was saying, "we truly would have been in danger had she stayed?"

"I honestly cannot say," he replied, releasing her from his embrace again, his strong hands finding their way to her shoulders now, "but I do know that the past cannot be changed, and we can only make choices in the present moment. I made my choices out of selfishness and pain; your mother made her choices from a place of self-sacrifice, love and hope."

"But you're not selfish now!" Martha said, it was a statement she knew to be true. This was a dream but somehow, she knew her dream father was every bit like her real father.

"No, I'm not." He said smiling, "I have indeed changed, in large part because your mother took you away! You will change too, over time, though I feel you already know more than I did."

"So, it's safe to find you now?" Martha asked, hopeful.

"We," he paused and looked thoughtful for a moment before he continued, "we will be together sooner than you think." He finally said.

"We will?" She said, excitement thrilled her.

"Yes." He said, quietly, another tear falling down his face.

"Why are you sad?" Martha asked. "Won't that be a good thing?"

"It will be a beautiful thing." He insisted. "But there is something you need to do first."

"What's that?" Martha asked.

"You know what it is, I told you before." He said with a sly smile.

"You did?" She was more confused now.

"Yes, and you don't remember, but you will when the time is right." He assured her. He held her hands in his and squeezed. "I love you, Martha. And I promise we will all be together again, a family, just as we were meant to be. Happy and loved."

"Promise?" Martha asked, skeptically.

"I promise." He insisted. "I will see you soon." He stood, walked away and was gone.

A trembling hand held hers and squeezed firmly but gently.

"Mary?" The voice was familiar and soft; her name was a whisper. Martha opened her eyes, Mama was holding her hand, as soon as Mama saw Martha's eyes looking up at her, tears fell freely from both of them. Mama leaned over and gently cradled Martha in her arms. Time was lost. Martha recalled the words of her father, saying that she was supposed to do something before they would be together again. She couldn't remember what it was. Mama was saying something now, but Martha couldn't focus on her words. She was too caught up in the dream she'd just had and now that she was awake the pain in her wrist was awful again, worse than before. She tried to ignore it. The last few days of pretending there was nothing wrong had become second nature. She wasn't sure how to act now.

Aunt Ruth came into the room then, Mama was sitting on the edge of the bed and Martha was propped up with the pillows, Aunt ruth ran to her side and hugged her tightly. The movement of being embraced pulled at Matha's right arm, making it move drastically, and she felt her arm convulse and tighten. The tightness in her arm stopped abruptly but was followed by tightness creeping up her jaw line. Too familiar, the pain in her muscles felt as though they were slowly winding up, preparing for something she didn't want to understand. She braced for the pain she knew was coming.

Stiffness in the back of her neck spread from her jaw and down, through her back. Her jaw twitched and she moved her tongue just before her teeth clamped down on themselves against her will. Like a fire running through a drought-ridden wheat field, tension and pain spread through her entire back and every other muscle in her body. The merciless blaze of agony seized every muscle it reached, her body was fighting against her and keeping her a prisoner in this anguish. Panic sprang when she realized she couldn't breathe. Her back arched and she felt something snap, a new wave of anguish shooting from her chest. She tried to scream, but the sound couldn't make it past the barrier in her throat. A person needed air to scream, and she didn't have any. Pinpricks of shadow danced across her vision and the edges of sight slowly dwindled. She was vaguely aware of people moving quickly around her but couldn't make sense of anything at all. Her vision was severely diminished now, and she couldn't see much at all. Just a tunnel directly in front of her. Her lungs burned; she needed air, the harder she fought to breathe, the more everything hurt, suddenly her back stopped arching and her whole body convulsed, and there was blackness.

"Not yet. Soon." Martha heard her father's voice in the distance but couldn't see anything. "Breathe, Martha. Breathe now!"

She gasped, and the world swam back into view. Pain radiated from the right side of her chest, but her lungs greedily gulped the air. Each inhale was followed by a screaming exhale. She was screaming. With each breath she screamed. The pain was too much! Everything hurt, burned and ached. Uncle Daniel was standing next to her trying to say something, but she didn't understand. Her screams were unbidden and unyielding, and the two nurses who had been here before were holding her arm down as Uncle Daniel held a syringe and drove it into her arm. She didn't even feel the needle. The pain in the rest of her body was too agonizing. The nurses let her arm go once Uncle Daniel had administered the injection. She kept breathing, and while the pain was still there it began to subside. The screams turned into unwelcome and haunting moans. Mama and Ruth were now standing in the corner of the room holding each other, tears streaking down their cheeks, then she realized she was crying too.

"That should help some, with the pain and the spasms." Uncle Daniel said, "keep your muscles relaxed as much as you can."

"Is she going to be alright?" Mama asked.

"Let's go into the hall to talk." Uncle Daniel said. His professional attitude clearly had snapped back into place after this episode.

"NO!" Martha shouted, the pain from the effort causing her to wince. "I want to hear."

"Are you sure?" Uncle Daniel asked.

"I need to know." She insisted.

"What do you think, Elizabeth?" He asked, turning to get approval from Mama.

"I think," Mama paused, looked at Martha and with a tear, "I think she needs to hear it. I watched my sister go through cancer and my parents wouldn't let us know anything. I wished they'd let us know, so If Mary wants to know what's happening to her, she deserves that, unfiltered."

Martha whispered, "thank you", then looked at Uncle Daniel.

"What's happening to me? What is this? It hurts so much."

"I'm afraid, you have tetanus." Uncle Daniel said, pulling the stool closer to the bed again. He took her left hand in his and asked, "you want to know everything?"

"Yes." Martha whispered, some uncertainty prickling against her consciousness, but she pushed it down.

Uncle Daniel looked up at Mama, when Mama nodded her approval for him to continue, he said, "I don't know how you hurt your hand, May said she wasn't sure, but without proper cleaning, you contracted tetanus."

Martha had heard of Tetanus, but never thought she would get it, especially with Uncle Daniel being a doctor.

"The other day, you came walking to the house, you had a severe fever, and I couldn't figure out why you were unconscious. My guess is that your body was shutting down. If May hadn't insisted that I look at your hand I think we would have lost you that night."

Martha was struggling to take this all in. Uncle Daniel was still holding her hand, he was being as professional as he could, but this man was clearly emotional about the whole ordeal, they loved each other as a real family would, and she knew how much she would miss him if anything had happened to him. She didn't say anything, the pain in her side was too much just from breathing, and talking seemed to make it worse.

"I brought you to the hospital as fast as I could. I put you in my car and drove faster than I realized was possible, if I hadn't, you wouldn't have made it through that first night." Uncle Daniel paused and wiped a tear from his eye before he continued. "We got you stabilized, and we did what we could for your hand, but the tissue and tendons were so damaged from the infection, we had to take it."

Martha looked down at her right hand, the pain from the movement dulled by the realization that her hand was not, in fact, balled up in a fist, but wasn't there at all. The rough bandage was there in place of her hand. The pain that came from her wrist was because they had taken her hand. She looked back at Uncle Daniel for more information. She hadn't expected that. She didn't know what she would learn but knowing she only had one hand now was not on her list of things she'd expected.

"After we took your hand, your symptoms seemed to improve. We gave you everything we could think of to fight the infection, and when you woke up earlier today, I was hoping we'd be in the clear. But" He paused and looked up at Mama, "Are you sure you want me to tell you this in front of her? It's more than a child should have to hear."

"Daniel, either you say it here or I'll tell her later," Mama said, "Only I don't know if I'd get through it. I've kept enough from her already." Did Mama know about the box?

Uncle Daniel continued to hold Marthas left hand with his right hand but motioned for Mama and Aunt Ruth to come closer. As they walked around the bed, Uncle Daniel held Mama's hand, and Aunt Ruth put an arm around Mama's shoulders while holding her other hand on top of Mama and Uncle Daniels.

"Alright," He breathed deeply and cleared his throat and made no move to wipe his tears this time, he let them fall freely. He nodded at the nurses that remained in the room and they left, closing the door behind them. "The tetanus is advanced enough that I am not sure we can actually treat it at all." His voice broke.

"What does that mean?" Mama asked, a quiver in her voice.

"It means," Aunt ruth said, after it looked like Uncle Daniel couldn't find the words; his tears were coming silently, but hard and fast and he was trying desperately to control them to no avail. "That the tetanus will likely take her life." She glanced at Martha, trying to seem brave and smiled weakly.

Uncle Daniel nodded and more tears fell. Aunt Ruth started crying in earnest too now, as did Mama. No one said a word, though everyone could feel the weight of what was just said. It had just been a dream then, nothing more. She wouldn't see her father; she wouldn't reunite Mama with him. They wouldn't be a family after all. It was all just her imagination. Her foolish dreams.

"How long do we have?" Mama asked.

"It's hard to tell," Uncle Daniel said, snapping back into Dr Mode. "Could be a few days, could be a couple of weeks at best." He stood and let the Dr mask fall enough to bend and kiss her forehead again. "All we can do is try to keep the spasms at bay and let her rest as comfortably as possible, but this last one sounded like she broke a rib."

Was that what that snapping sound had been? She didn't dare move as Uncle Daniel reached around and gingerly felt her rib cage. His gentle fingers brushing along the ribs until, "OW!" And tears sprang from Martha's eyes.

"Definitely a broken rib." He said. "It doesn't seem to be affecting her breathing at all but compounded with the tetanus we will keep a very close eye on that. I'll have oxygen for her in case she needs it, and I won't leave here unless I absolutely have to.

"Is there anything we can do to help her pain levels?" Mama asked.

"There's not much we can do." He said. "I gave her morphine as soon as I heard the snap, but that's not the best thing to do either with tetanus. You saw how she was going blue, the spasm blocked off her airways and she couldn't breathe. I gave her the morphine as it was the closest thing I had on hand, it was a very small dose and I don't dare give her anymore, it could stop her breathing altogether."

"So there's nothing we can do, nothing at all?" Mama said as Aunt Ruth held her firmly, crying and unable to speak.

"I can sedate her; I think that would be best." He spoke softly as though he weren't sure Martha could handle much more.

"I agree." Martha spoke up, despite the pain. She didn't know how long she would be alive, and according to Aunt Ruth, it wouldn't be long. But if she could sleep through most of it, that would be ideal.

"Are you sure?" Mama said, more tears streaming down her face.

"I'm sure." Martha said, "Would I be asleep the whole time?"

"No," Said Uncle Daniel, "we would give you sedatives then once they wear off, we would feed you and make sure you're comfortable before giving you more."

"Could I please see May and Suzie?" Martha asked. She knew that if she was truly dying, she had to see them one more time.

"Of course!" Aunt Ruth choked through tears. Mama nodded yes as well.

"Not today," Uncle Daniel asserted, "You'll be sleeping soon. That morphine will help you sleep."

Martha noticed that she did feel more relaxed and somewhat tired now that he mentioned it. She nodded slightly, then looked at the three adults standing next to her bed. Even though it had just been a dream, her father was right. She couldn't blame anyone in this room, least of all her mother. Everything she had ever known her to do was completely out of love for her and for those around her. Looking at her now, she truly recognized the love and gratitude that seemed to follow Mama everywhere. Whatever happened, even if she would never get to meet her father, or know anyone else in her family, she needed this family to know she loved and appreciated them.

"I love you all so much," the words came from Martha as no more than a whisper, "I hope you know that."

They all looked at her, no one in the room had dry eyes. "Love you too!" They each said over top of one another. One by one, first Uncle Daniel, then Aunt Ruth and finally Mama, bent over and kissed her head. Her eyes became heavy, and she drifted off into a deep sleep.

Chapter 15

Her father didn't visit her in her dreams this time. She wondered if she'd ever see his face again. She had given up hope of finding him in life and the thought of even seeing him in her dreams seemed unlikely with drug induced sleep. She wasn't aware of time passing and hadn't any awareness of anything happening around her as she slept. There was a moment of lucidity just before she fell asleep, as Mama and the others left the room and she resigned herself to her fate. She would die. That was the end of it. The end of her. She would no longer exist. All she had hoped for, dreamed of, was now gone. The only person to blame for this was herself. She had made the choice to break open that box, and not to tell Mama or Aunt Ruth about hurting her hand. What if she had? Would things be different now?

She was aware briefly of waking up for a few minutes, the sky outside was dark. Her body ached. She wanted to stretch but as she tried to adjust, sharp pain from her side caused her to cry out in agony and dictated she not move at all. She realized she had been wrapped up in some sort of tight bandage around her ribs. The door to her room opened, it was Uncle Daniel.

"Hi sweetie," he said, "Just in time. I'll have someone bring you some broth before we sedate you."

She couldn't think of anything to say, so she just nodded in agreement. He left the room, and a few minutes later a new nurse came in, and helped her to drink some strong broth. Not long after that, Uncle Daniel came back in with a syringe.

"This will help you sleep the rest of the night," He said as he administered the drug, "Love you, Mary."

"You need sleep too." She said in a hoarse whisper.

"I'll go home once I know you're resting." He assured her. "I'll be back before you're awake."

"But" she couldn't think of what she actually wanted to say. The medicine was already making her head swim.

"I'll make sure someone is listening for you constantly." He insisted, then he kissed her forehead. He didn't leave the room.

Her eyes grew heavier, and the blissful weight of sleep overtook her again. No time. No awareness. No pain.

Until there was. Sharp, agonizing pain radiated through her, her eyes popped open, and she gasped for breath, she was laying on her side, laying on the side with the broken rib. She cried out, screamed out.

"I'm so sorry dear," an unfamiliar voice said, "we're almost done."

Hands were on her back and thigh; someone was changing pads underneath her. Tears and moans simultaneously escaped from her. She was trying to hold still but the pain was unbearable. She heard the door open, another nurse had come in.

"What are you doing?" The new voice said, angrily, "She has a broken rib on that side!" The angry voice turned to a harsh whisper as the new voice realized that Martha was awake and in pain. She chastised the other nurses and quickly helped lay Martha back down as gently as possible before shooing the others out. "Oh, my dear," she said, wiping hair from Martha's face, "I'm so sorry. You weren't supposed to be changed until later. You weren't even supposed to be awake yet. Dr Abernathy won't be in for another hour.

I'll be right back." she said, covering Martha with an extra blanket before she left the room.

Matha lay still, trying not to think about the pain radiating through her entire body. She tried to relax and did her best to stay calm. She breathed deeply and focused on the gift that air was. She concentrated on pulling that air in and out of her lungs for a few minutes. She remembered too well the fear that she had yesterday when she wasn't able to breathe at all. As she took another breath, the now familiar tightness started in her jaw. The tightness spread through her neck. She wasn't stiff or incapacitated yet, and now, she knew she needed to speak up.

"Help!" She shouted as loudly as she could, she was rewarded with more pain from the effort. "Help!" She shouted again, just before her jaw was too tight to open it again. A groan escaped from her chest just as the door opened and the nurse that had helped her minutes ago came in with a doctor, it wasn't Uncle Daniel.

"She's having another spasm." The Dr. Said as he rushed to her side. "Grab the sedative now." He held Martha's arm firmly.

"Just breathe. Keep breathing." She looked up at the doctor to acknowledge him, but he hadn't said it. "Just breathe." She heard again. The voice was clear as day and peaceful. She breathed and let the words calm her. "Breathe." The voice said again. She did.

The nurse came back with a syringe in less than a minute. Martha could feel tightness spreading down her neck and into her back, another moan. Fear crept in as she felt the tightness encircle her chest, her broken rib started grinding against its other half. "Everything is going to be all right."

She heard the voice say. "Keep breathing." She did her best to obey.

A few more breaths and the tightness began to ease slightly. She looked at the doctor, he had already given her the medicine. It felt different than the medicine that Uncle Daniel had given her. A strange and welcoming warmth spread from her arm and through the rest of her body. Everywhere it spread she relaxed. Another syringe was produced from somewhere Martha didn't know or care. Before she knew it, she was fading off again. Blessed reprieve.

Her eyes fluttered open again, her body stiff from not moving for who knew how many hours. Light streamed through the window again. The sheer curtains filtered the soft yellow light. It must be either early morning or late afternoon. Not wanting to make any noise for fear of causing pain in her rib, she just breathed shallowly and enjoyed the gentle warmth of the space. As she lay there, she wondered vaguely about how it would feel to die. It couldn't hurt more than what she'd already felt the last few weeks. There wasn't enough time. She knew that. Not enough time to do anything, especially when she couldn't get out of this bed. She heard the door open, but she didn't dare turn to see who was there.

"You're awake." A cheery voice said. Martha didn't respond, she was too tired to, she just kept looking toward the window. "Let's get you something to eat." She said. Again, Martha didn't respond.

The nurse left and came back a few minutes later with a tray full of food. Martha was sure it smelled fine, but the other smells from the hospital were still attacking her senses and she didn't want to eat, but she swallowed every bite the nurse put in her mouth. Each time she chewed she worried it would cause her body to go into a spasm. Every time she swallowed, she was worried it would hurt. She didn't spasm though, and her pain never increased dramatically. She was grateful for that. She vaguely wondered where Uncle Daniel was, he had said he'd be here. She didn't want to ask though, she felt selfish wanting him there when she knew he had other family to worry about, other patients. He also needed rest. So, she said nothing. Just ate the food the nurse put in her mouth, her eyes never wandering from the curtains. At length, she couldn't make herself open her mouth for another bite. She felt as though she would be sick and lose everything she'd eaten if she swallowed one more mouthful. She couldn't find words, so she just turned her head ever so slightly away from the fork when it was raised to her mouth.

"I'll go call Dr. Abernathy." The nurse said as she placed the fork back onto the tray. She stood and left the room.

Martha stared at the drapes. Was this the rest of her life? Sitting in this bed until she stopped existing? She didn't want to die, but she couldn't see the use of existing like this. The realization hit her that yes. This would indeed be the rest of her life.

The door opened and the nurse came back in. She let Martha know that Dr. Abernathy was on the way. She asked if Martha was comfortable. She asked if Martha needed anything. There were no words to be found.

She closed her eyes, how was she so tired even though she had been unconscious for so long? She focused on her slow breathing and drifted to sleep as she waited for something to happen.

The room was the same as last time. The walls that were comforting and felt like home, but she couldn't focus on them. The soft, luxurious purple sofa with an ornately carved wooden frame. She was sitting on the sofa, and she instinctively looked around for someone, for her father. She didn't see him or anyone. She stood and walked around the room. She wanted to take it in. There were more seats than she had realized before. Multiple sofas and armchairs that matched the one she had been sitting on. A dark wooden table sat in the center of the room; it was round and matched the wood on the sofas and chairs. A large bouquet in a masterfully crafted crystal vase sat on the table. She wondered how she had missed all these things before. The bouquet was so big that she had to tilt her head up slightly to see the top of it, as she did, she saw that there was a chandelier above it; more intricate and beautiful than she could have ever imagined one being. As she allowed herself to be swept away by the beauty of the piece, she heard a soft, "Martha." She turned to see a woman. She was familiar and yet not. She was the same woman Martha had seen in her dream with the mist. The woman who'd told her it wasn't time. The woman was sitting on the same sofa that her father and she had sat on before.

These dreams always felt so real when she was having them, and she wished they didn't have to end. Martha crossed the room and sat next to the woman.

"Who are you?" That was all Martha could think of asking.

"Do you not know?" was the woman's reply, she had a sweet and slightly mischievous smile.

Martha thought for a moment, looking deeply in her eyes and realization hit, then she whispered, "You're my father's mother." The woman smiled broadly all love and beauty, "My grandmother!" she said more confidently.

The woman held out her arms, Martha slid closer and embraced her. She let the feeling of love she felt from this woman, the woman she had known was her grandmother, permeate her entire being.

"You knew I was dying before," Martha said as she pulled away from the embrace, "you knew it, why didn't you tell me?"

"You weren't ready to hear it then." Grandmother said.

"I am ready now." Martha said. "I'm ready to die now."

"You are?" Grandmother asked.

"Yes." Martha said, then her resolve failed, "and no."

"Then you are not ready." Grandmother said, placing a hand on Martha's knee.

"Will I ever be ready?" Martha asked, choking up on the last word.

"You'll know when you're ready." Grandmother's words were comforting.

"Will it hurt?" Martha asked.

"No. Dying doesn't hurt. Sometimes there's pain before dying, but the dying itself never hurts." Grandmother's words made sense but were confusing at the same time.

"My father told me I'd see him soon. But he was wrong." Martha said, tears now forming. "He said that my mother, he, and I would be a family. But I'm dying. It will never happen now."

"Won't it?" Grandmother's question came with knowing behind it.

"How can it? I'm nearing the end." Martha whispered.

"The end of what, Dear?" grandmother asked with that mischievous smile again. Then she winked.

"The end of everything!" Martha said, a tear formed in her eye.

"Hmm." Grandmother said, infinite knowing in her eyes. "You, your mother and your father being a family? Is that what you want?"

"Yes!" Martha responded without hesitation.

"Would that make you happy?" Grandmother asked.

"More than anything!" Tears fell from Martha's eye now, but grandmother swept them up with her thumb. Her touch was soft, gentle and warm. It felt so real! But she knew she was dreaming.

"It can happen, and it will. I'll be there too!" Her eyes sparkled.

"How?" Martha wasn't sure why these dreams kept tormenting her. They were a welcome reprieve from the pain and anguish of her waking life, but so heartbreaking when she woke, knowing that this kind of peace wasn't real. That whatever this was, whatever place she was in where she could see and hear and talk to her father and now her grandmother, it was all in her imagination.

"The 'how' is very important, though I'm not sure I can fully explain it, even now." Grandmother smiled sweetly.

"I don't understand." Martha wished that dream grandmother, in her youthful beauty, would give her some actual advice or insight, instead of just making her more confused.

"Do you really think that you just end when you die? That the life you've known and lived is all there is?" Grandmother asked. She leaned over and hugged Martha gently, and whispered in her ear, "Soon, there will be no more pain for you. We will be together soon. Just not yet. Don't be afraid. You're not alone. Now, go!"

Chapter 16

Martha opened her eyes, it was dark outside again, and Uncle Daniel was standing next to her bed.

"I heard you ate some dinner!" He said, looking pleased. "You ate much more than I thought you would be able to. That's good!"

"How long do I have left?" she asked. "Be honest with me."

"Mary," he said, taking her hand, "that's hard to say. Your body is going through a lot right now. It could be a while; it could be less than a day. You could make a miraculous recovery!"

"But I won't." She said matter-of-factly.

"No," He frowned. "You likely won't."

"Uncle Daniel," She needed to ask, "What happens after we die?"

He looked taken aback. "I'm not sure. No one really knows." He paused with a thoughtful expression on his face and then added, "but I know that your Aunt Ruth has felt strongly that we keep going on afterward."

"How does she know that?" she asked.

"I don't think she knows, but she believes. She believes it deeply." He said.

"What if she's wrong?" Martha challenged.

"What if she's right?" Uncle Daniel rebutted.

"I hope she's right." She really did.

"I hope so too!" Uncle Daniel agreed.

They stayed that way for a long time, Uncle Daniel holding her hand as they both looked at the drapes and that dark sky beyond them. There was so much more that Martha hoped for, wanted to know. But she also knew that she wouldn't get any of it now. Not from anyone she knew.

"It's been an eventful day," he said at length, "are you ready to sleep some more?"

Marhta nodded yes. He left the room then came back in with a syringe. She felt the warm drowsiness spread from her arm and through her shoulder, into her back.

"Can I see people tomorrow?" Martha asked as she felt her last word turn mushy in her mouth.

"We will try again for certain." Uncle Daniel said.

"Try again?" Martha asked, bleary eyed.

"Yes." He replied. "Everyone was here earlier, but you were very much asleep. Hopefully tonight you'll be allowed to sleep so you can see them tomorrow."

She closed her eyes and that was all she knew.

When she opened her eyes, the light was muted from outside. Martha turned her head toward the sheer fabric flowing from the windows. The snow was coming down fast and hard, if she could see it through the sheer curtains, she knew it was bad. An involuntary shiver ran down her spine as she imagined the cold.

A nurse came in; Martha wasn't sure if she'd seen her before or not. She realized that she had been so focused on the prospect of death the last few days that her short moments of being wake were not as pleasant as she would want people to remember her. She made an effort to smile at the nurse.

"Good afternoon, miss Jones." The nurse said when she noticed Martha smiling. "How are you feeling? Hungry?"

Martha's throat felt dry so she didn't try to speak, but realized she should probably eat, a nod yes and a broader smile was her response.

"Good!" The nurse said finishing up her task, "I'll go get you something to eat and let Dr. Abernathy know you're up."

The nurse left the room and pulled the door behind her, but rather than close completely, the door bounced open a few inches instead of latching. As the door swung slowly open, it was just enough for Martha to see in the hallway. There was nothing spectacular, nothing at all. Just an empty hall and she could see another door across from hers. She could hear voices talking down the hall, she assumed it was nurses and other doctors. What caught her attention though, was the sounds coming from the room across the hall, muffled and quiet, but distinct. The people in that room were crying. She knew that sound, it was the same sound she'd made when she'd learned about her father. The sound of grief and loss. Somone had died in that room, just across the hall from her. She listened as their sobs grew louder, softer and then louder again, going from whimpers to howls. She had been so caught up in her own situation that she hadn't even thought about anyone else possibly fighting for life in this same building. She felt humbled and sick to her stomach. How many people were struggling every day that she wasn't even aware of? Suzie had been struggling for a long time over losing her father, and all it had taken was one person taking a moment to try to understand what she was feeling, and Suzie was now a completely different person.

"Mary," Uncle Daniel whispered as he entered the room alone and rushed to her bed, quickly wiping a tear from her cheek, "What's happened?" He asked.

She hadn't even realized she'd started crying, she tried to speak in response but the lump in her throat prevented words from forming. She lifted a finger and pointed through the open door to the sounds that were so strong now she could feel them as well as hear them. Uncle Daniel paused, and looked behind him, seeing the open door he hurried to close it.

"No, don't!" Martha said through muted tears, "They shouldn't grieve alone." He smiled and closed the door most of the way, leaving it open only an inch, she assumed more for their privacy than her protection. He grabbed the stool and pulled it to her bedside sitting with her, neither of them speaking. Just listening and Uncle Daniel started crying with the people across the hall too, mourning with them in quiet solidarity.

The nurse knocked on the door giving them just enough time to dry their eyes before she came in and rested a food tray on a table next to the bed.

"Thank you, nurse Hampton," Uncle Daniel said, "I'll help her from here."

The nurse left, closing the door completely behind her, the finality that the clicking of the latch brought felt deeply personal to Martha. The moment it closed, the crying from across the hall was silenced and couldn't be heard at all. It was so quiet; as though it had never happened. Was that what was going to happen to her? Once she died, would people cry for a while then forget about her? One last tear fell.

Uncle Daniel stayed with her as she ate, after a few bites she realized how tired her arms were, and she asked if he wouldn't mind helping her eat a little more. After he helped her finish eating all she could, which admittedly wasn't much, he said, "Everyone is going to try to come by a bit later, but with the snow there's no guarantee. I can sedate you now or we can wait for a while and see if they can make it, you decide."

"I'd like to see them if they can come." She said. "I'm a little tired though, would it be alright if I slept on my own?"

"Yes," he said, "I'll have a nurse stationed close to keep an ear out for you." She nodded and he took the tray of food out of the room with him.

"Wait!" Marhta said just before closed the door again, "Promise me you'll wake me up if they come?"

"I promise." And he closed the door, leaving her alone.

The room was eerily still and quiet after the soft noise from the grieving occupants across the hall, she strained her ears to see if she could catch any hint of them, but it was useless. They'd either stopped crying or left the room. There was only silence. Such complete silence after such heart wrenching sounds, it unnerved her. The finality that she was facing along with the far too brief life she'd led suddenly felt so real. Her thoughts turned to her mother and her surrogate family. She loved Uncle Daniel, Aunt Ruth, May and all the boys dearly. She was more grateful for them than they probably knew, but it wasn't the same as her blood family. Knowing that so many of them were already dead, knowing that Mama had no idea what happened to them, left her feeling more alone than just sitting in an empty hospital room. What was worse, no one else knew she existed. Her own Father had no idea he even had a child, a daughter.

Would anyone but her mother express grief at her loss for more than a few days? Or would she be completely forgotten with no one to claim her as theirs?

She closed her eyes, hoping her exhaustion would allow her to sleep of her own accord rather than being in a drug-induced sleep. Laying there, propped up on pillows in her hospital room, she became acutely aware of her muscles. She hadn't had a spasm for a while, but her muscles ached. The fatigue she felt from simply trying to eat left her more tired than she'd expected. She did her best to relax and hoped for sleep to overcome her. She did her best to ignore the stiffness of her joints and muscles. She closed her eyes and after what felt like an eternity, she was back in the room with the purple sofas and the chandelier.

She sat and waited for someone to come to her. No one did. She walked around the table with the bouquet of flowers, noticing that she had no idea what these flowers were. Exotic colors and vivid smells filled her with hope. She walked around the room looking up at the chandelier appreciating the ornate craftsmanship. Still, no one else came into the room. She stepped further to the edges of the room now, to get a better view of the chandelier above. She bumped into a chair behind her, and turned to see it was up against the wall, the wall she couldn't focus on before, was beautiful too! The wallpaper was white, cream and eggshell, intricately designed with curving vines and sprawling leafy organics with an occasional muted purple or washed-out green accent. The white, curved, hand carved wood pillar details around the edge of the wall where it met the high ceiling were breathtakingly beautiful and matched the carvings on the wood from the furniture perfectly. She noticed that the framework around the doors was also an exact match. Doors? She hadn't even noticed doors before. She reasoned that in dreams, doors aren't necessary, she hadn't used a door to get here herself. There were four doors: single doors on the left and right of the room, tall, white and ornate with gold hardware, also carved and intricate. Sets of double doors were at the front and back of the room, these too were white, but less ornately decorated and had silver hardware. She assumed that the differences between the doors were significant but didn't dwell on it much.

She walked to one of the single doors and reached for the handle, just as she reached for it but before she could touch it, it turned. She took a step back as the door opened and her father entered the room. "It's not time yet." He said, tears filling his eyes. "I'm so sorry, but this will be difficult."

He left the door behind him open, and Martha looked behind him watching the door, as he walked to stand beside her, and she saw a woman enter the room as well, her grandmother. "Hello, dear." She said as she entered the room and closed the door behind her.

They walked, all three of them, over to sit on one of the sofas, Martha in the middle, her father on her left and her grandmother on her right.

"It's almost time." Grandmother said.

"But not quite yet." Father finished.

"Time?" Martha asked. What were they talking about?

"Yes." Grandmother said, tears were now filling her eyes too. "Nearly, but you need to be strong until then."

"It's going to get much harder first." Father said, empathy flooding his face. "Remember that you're not alone."

"We will be with you every step of the way, even if you don't see us." Grandmother said.

"And others, too." Father interjected, he smiled even with the tears and sadness on his face, she saw joy there. "You will never be alone."

"Isn't there anything I can do?" Martha asked. She wasn't ready to die; she realized that that was what they were talking about.

"Only one thing." Father said, "The thing you need to remember to do, what I asked you to do before." He said, grabbing her hand and squeezing it.

"But I can't remember what that was!" Martha said, guilt flooding through her. She couldn't remember and had forgotten about it the moment she woke up from the last dream in which she had seen him.

"You will," he assured her, "when the time is right, you will."

"And remember, you won't be alone." Grandmother said standing up. She held her hand out to Martha and helped her stand.

Hand in hand, grandmother led her to the double doors at one end of the room. She didn't know why, but she knew she didn't want to go through them.

"Can't I stay here with you?" Martha asked.

"No. You must go back." Grandmother said, hugging her tightly before reaching for the silver doorknob. She turned it and gently and lovingly guided Martha through the door.

Martha's eyes opened and the dream was gone; she was back in her hospital bed. Her legs stiff and sore, she tried to flex her feet, but they didn't want to move. Her jaw was tight, and she couldn't bring her aching arm up to brush the sweat from her brow. Closing her eyes to try to sleep some more, she was interrupted by the door opening. Looking to the left with only her eyes, her neck was too stiff to turn, she saw Uncle Daniel come into the room and shadowy figures in the hallway behind him. He closed the door and came close to the bed.

His smile was beaming; he grabbed a handkerchief from his pocket and wiped the sweat from her face without a word. He stood and smiled at her for a long time, she guessed he was trying to ascertain how she was feeling. She didn't interrupt him.

"Are you feeling up for visitors?" he asked after a few minutes. Was that who was in the hallway?

She smiled, and a whispered "Yes." Was all that that came out. Her jaw ached when she tried to move it and even her tongue felt tired.

He stepped away from the bed and opened the door, standing behind it so he didn't block her view. Mama, Aunt Ruth, May, Scott, Deryk, Grayson and Morgan were all there. After they came into the room, all smiles and awkward silence, there was still a shadowy person standing in the hall, Martha couldn't make out who it was.

"It's alright, come, come in." Uncle Daniel urged.

The figure took a few steps toward the door. They didn't enter the room but stood just beyond the doorframe, enough though that Martha could see it was Suzie. She wasn't crying, but Martha could see that she had been fighting tears for a while. Martha locked eyes with her, and in that moment, without any words or gestures, she understood that the last time Suzie had been inside a hospital was when her father had died.

"It's ok if you can't." Martha choked her words through her teeth; she sounded hoarse and ragged.

Her words must have given Suzie the strength she needed, because then Suzie practically ran into the room and to her side. Suzie threw her arms and upper body across Martha, a strange but meaningful hug. Martha could tell that Suzie instinctively knew that trying to give a proper hug would hurt her, so she did the best she could. Human contact was everything! Martha hadn't had a hug in days, and she hadn't realized how much she needed it. Suzie's body began to shudder, and Martha realized she was finally crying. Silent sobs shook her whole frame. Martha, with all the strength she had, lifted her left hand, and brought it to rest on Suzie's head.

"It'll be ok." Martha whispered. Her strength was nearly gone. She was so tired.

Suzie stood, "I'm so sorry."

Martha smiled and looked around the room at everyone else.

"I love you all so much." She said, making sure to look at each person here in the eye.

One by one, they each followed Suzie's lead and gave Martha an odd half hug, and Martha drank in every single one. First, Grayson, then Scott. Morgan was next and then Deryk. Aunt Ruth trailed him, then Mama hugged her the longest. Tears streamed down her face. Finally, May followed suit and hugged her tightly. May was stalwart and strong; the only one without any sign of a tear. Martha appreciated her strength; she needed it, and it was a salve for her heart. May stood from the hug and then leaned forward to whisper in her ear.

"We heard back about your father." She said in such a soft tone that Martha wasn't sure if she'd heard it correctly. When May pulled back to full standing again, Martha knew she hadn't been mistaken.

Marha's eyes widened, and with effort and a wince she turned her head slightly to look at May more closely. At this moment, Suzie walked to stand next to May so Marhta could see them both. Suzie must have either known or guessed what May had said. Martha's eyes widened, afraid to hope. Then she noticed the looks on her friends' faces. May was still wearing her stalwart expression and Suzie looked as though she may start crying again at any moment.

"Tell me." Martha plead.

May and Suzie looked at everyone else in the room as though they were uncertain whether they should say anything in front of them. Mama and Aunt Ruth looked concerned but didn't say anything. They could tell something was going on but didn't want to interrupt. Martha knew that whatever her friends had to say wasn't good, and felt that whatever it was, Mama should know and there might not be another chance to let her hear it. May and Suzie wouldn't say anything to Mama after Martha was gone.

Suzie and May looked at each other, still hesitant. They looked at Aunt Ruth and Mama, then back at each other.

"Please." Martha choked out. Her jaw felt stiffer and stiffer. The pain in her ribs nearly brought her to tears, if she wasn't full of dreaded anticipation she may have fallen apart right then.

"Ok," Suzie said at last, "I sent that letter to my uncle in California."

"What letter?" Mama interrupted; the word California had brought visible distress to her.

"Mary found her birth certificate." May said, glancing at the adults without making eye contact.

"She WHAT?" Mama said. "You what?" She asked a second time, this time addressing Martha directly. "How?"

Martha couldn't answer. May would have to fill her in later. Martha looked from Mama back to Suzie and May, urging with her eyes for them to continue.

"I sent the letter," Suzie continued, "I hadn't heard anything at all, I Wasn't even sure if he'd gotten my letter. But after I heard you were in the hospital and how sick you were…" Suzie stopped talking and began to cry. Martha needed to know but had no strength to comfort her friend or convince her to continue.

May stepped closer to Suzie and put an arm around her. "After I told her what had happened to you," May continued, "Suzie went home that day and arranged for her mother to call her uncle. He's a big Lawyer in California. So, her mother called and got in touch with him while he was at his office and arranged for a time when Suzie could call and talk to him."

"I was able to talk to him just yesterday." Suzie said between sobs. "I told him everything. That you'd gotten hurt, that you were sick, and you wanted to find your father before… before you…" Suzie started crying again, so fervently that Mama stepped forward. Martha thought Mama would be furious, but instead, she reached out and embraced Suzie with all the love she had.

May let Mama take care of Suzie, "She told him everything about you. How you wanted to find him before it was too late." May avoided the word death. "He said he knew him, Mary. Suzie's uncle knew your father!"

"Knew?" Martha asked. The past tense of the word wasn't lost on her.

May nodded, then stared at the floor.

"I'm so sorry." Suzie said, crying harder now. She grasped at Mama's back; she must have been feeling the loss of her own father so fresh now.

Martha didn't know how to respond. Fresh grief rose in her chest too. "When?" She finally said, the word dry and crackly.

"Just over two months ago." May said with finality.

Silence filled the room to overflowing and it threatened to deafen Martha. She looked at Mama, whose eyes were shiny with tears of grief now too.

"How?" Mama asked, breaking the silence at last.

"I didn't think to ask." Suzie said, looking up at her, regret in her eyes. Mama didn't respond, she just gave a sad and understanding smile and hugged Suzie tighter.

The world swam around Martha, her head felt dizzy, and the room suddenly felt smaller. Her father really was gone. There would be no way to see him, find him, let him know anything that she had done in her too short life.

Her jaw felt tighter unexpectedly. It was another spasm, she knew it. "HELP!" She said as best she could to Uncle Daniel. Her jaw was already clenching, the familiar and hated sensation of tightening muscles threatened to choke her. She watched as Uncle Daniel ushered everyone from the room as quickly as he could, calling for a nurse to bring him something at the same time. Her chest grew tighter and her back began to arch slightly as the nurse rushed in with a syringe. The welcome stabbing sensation from the needle meant that she would soon be unaware of anything. She now welcomed the oncoming oblivion, but it wasn't coming fast enough. She let out a small scream unintentionally as the spasm arched her back more, going through her legs and the muscles pulled at her broken rib. She didn't want Mama or the others to hear how bad this was. She couldn't do that to them. She tried to be silent, but whimpers of agony escaped quietly as wet eyes leaked down her face and into her hair. The edges of her vision began to blur as the medicine slowly seeped through her body. Why was this happening to her? How could she possibly endure more pain? She wondered. Just before everything went black, she thought she saw her father standing in the corner of the hospital room.

Chapter 17

Time was irrelevant and made no sense. Martha woke periodically; there was always a nurse nearby now. Once she woke up, they would immediately try to help her eat, but after a few tries, she found it hard to swallow. She would never eat again. Uncle Daniel ordered an IV therapy tube to be placed. The nurses brought in a glass bottle with a clear solution inside it, a tube protruded from the cork. She was given another sedative and was unconscious before they attached the tubing to her arm.

From time to time she would wake, look around the room and once a nurse noticed she was awake, they would try to ask questions, "How are you feeling?" or "Is there anything I can do to make you more comfortable?" After a few days, speaking was such a chore that Martha stopped trying. Every muscle hurt; every joint was stiff. There was no reprieve from the pain. Then she would be sedated again. Sometimes when she woke up, she would see Uncle Daniel, a few times she saw Mama. When Mama was there, she was alone. She would be sitting in a chair next to the bed, holding Martha's left hand tightly in her own.

Once, Martha opened her eyes to see Mama reading a book. She had never seen this book before. It was a black book that appeared to be leather bound. The front cover said Holy Bible. Somehow, she felt comforted by it and needed to know why. Mama hadn't noticed that she had opened her eyes yet, and she needed to say something. She breathed in as much as she could and choked out, "What's that?"

Mama nearly dropped the book.

"My sweet girl!" Mama said, standing from her chair and placing the book open, pages down, on the seat. "How are you?"

Martha just smiled and looked at the book with her eyes. Mama followed her gaze, smiled when she saw what she was looking and a looked back to Martha with understanding.

"That is the Bible, Martha." Mama looked as though she had done something wrong. She could see guilt flooding her face.

"Mama, I love you." Martha didn't know why Mama looked so sad and guilty, but she knew that her mother hadn't done anything to hurt her.

"That book, used to be my favorite book to read." Mama said, wiping a stray tear from the corner of her eye. "I read it all the time. I read it to my sister sometimes. After she…" Mama's voice broke, and she had to take a deep breath. "After I lost my sister, I couldn't bring myself to read it again. I never got rid of it, but I never opened it. I kept it hidden in the box under my bed." Mama looked deep into Martha's eyes, no condemnation there, just understanding. "I went home to look at your birth certificate, and everything else. I'd forgotten it was in there."

"Why didn't you read it again?" Speaking was such a difficult task; it drained her energy. But she truly wanted to know about this book that gave her comfort just from looking at the cover.

"Because I think I was angry at God." Mama said.

"God?" Martha asked in her hoarse voice.

"I blamed him for taking her, my sister."

Martha plead with her eyes for more, and she hoped Mama understood.

"I've never talked about God or faith before, my love, I think because I didn't realize how much I still blamed Him for the bad things that happened in my life." Mama seemed to know what Martha always needed, even if she couldn't say it. Mama continued, "But after Suzie and May talked about you finding our birth certificate I had to know more. So, I looked at everything in the box, and when I found my Bible again, I felt so much love from God in that moment and I realized that He never left me, even though I thought he had. He brought me here, to Ruth and Daniel. He gave me you!" Mama bent down and kissed Martha on the forehead.

"Will you read it to me?" Martha asked, a feeling of hope flared inside her for the first time in her waking hours since being in the hospital.

"Of course!" Mama smiled.

Mama sat down and started reading, not from the beginning of the book, which Martha thought was strange, but Mama flipped to somewhere in the middle and began to read, Martha listened intently. It was a story about a little girl who was sick and dying. Her father had run to find a man named Jesus. When Jesus had finally come the girl had already died, Mama started crying at that part but kept reading. Jesus had called the girl back, saying, "Daughter, arise!" And the girl had woken from her sleep and was healed. Peace filled Martha and she closed her eyes. She heard Uncle Daniel come in then but didn't open her eyes or say anything. She welcomed the medicine that brought the oblivion but now she would look forward to hearing more stories about this man named Jesus.

Most of the time, Martha was put back under sedation before she could go into another spasm. Sometimes they weren't fast enough. She broke three more ribs during one particularly bad spasm. Twice, she spasmed while she was sedated, and the pain was so excruciating she was woken from unconsciousness. On two occasions, when she felt most alone, she would catch a glimpse of her father standing in the corner of her room while she was awake.

Some days were better than others and Mama would read more stories. Jesus was always in them. Talking about His father in heaven, God. Jesus performed miracles and healed the sick. He even called His friend Lazarus back from the dead. And in between those times, Martha would be thrown into fits of pain interspersed with black nothingness.

One day, as she opened her eyes, her body particularly tired, and drained, everything stiff from her neck to her toes, she saw her mother next to her. Mama was sitting in the chair, which was pushed right up next to the bed, she was holding Martha's left hand in her right hand, her head was lying on the edge of the bed and her left arm was draped over Martha's legs. Mama was sound asleep, and the Bible lay near Martha's feet. She wondered briefly if Mama had been reading her storied from the Bible while Martha slept.

Martha's chest felt tighter than it had ever felt before, and she wasn't sure how long she could keep fighting this battle she knew she was losing. She looked down at Mama, sleeping so peacefully and she knew she hadn't slept peacefully in a very long time. If only Martha could close her eyes and be at peace, truly. How could she leave Mama and May though? Tightening in her jaw came abruptly and began to spread through her neck, down her chest and into her belly. Her legs stiffened and her feet bent in odd directions. Her back didn't arch this time, but the muscles were all restricting at once. She looked up and saw her father, not just a glimpse of a shadow as before, but seemed so solid and real. Marth wanted to ask him questions, but she hadn't been able to speak clearly for days.

He walked from the corner of the room and laid his right hand on her stumpy bandaged wrist. The weight of it surprised her. He was real! She could feel him and see him. He was here. This, she knew, was no dream. He smiled softly, knowingly. She looked down at Mama, she wished she would wake up so she could see him. Her father, Mama's true love. Her heart ached for it, but she knew intuitively that Mama would not be able to see him if she did wake now. She glanced at the Bible and remembered the stories Mama had just read about Angels and more peace flooded her.

"It's nearly time now." Father said.

"Really?" Martha whispered without effort. Mama didn't stir.

"Nearly," he replied, "do you remember now?"

She looked back down at Mama, the stiffness seemed to lessen now, she could move her head slightly. "I do, but I don't know if I can." She said looking back at her father. "I don't want to hurt her."

"It will help her." Father replied.

"She will be so sad." She said, crying now. "I don't want to make her cry."

"Not saying anything will leave her crying more." He insisted.

"I don't know if I can do this." She whispered in such a small voice; she almost didn't hear it herself.

"You can." He squeezed her shoulder. "I'm right here."

"Ok," Martha whispered, a new conviction coming over her. She didn't know what to think or how to feel right now, she only knew that her father was right. If Mama woke to find her gone, her grief alone could kill her. But if she could say goodbye, say all the things she knew she needed to say, Mama would still be sad, but she would have hope. Hope that Martha herself hadn't had until now. Hope that this truly wasn't the end.

"Mama." Martha said, clearly. More clearly than she had been able to speak for a long time. Her voice felt and sounded strong. There was no hoarseness. Mama didn't move at first. Her father still stood beside her, with his left hand on her shoulder, he moved his right hand and placed it on her upper arm. He nodded. Martha picked up her arm, somehow it was easier to move now, the stiffness in her joints was less now too. She placed her bandaged arm on Mama's head, gently brushing the hair back away from her face.

"Mama," Martha repeated.

Mama startled awake, "Mary, baby!" she exclaimed, "You're awake!"

"Mama, I love you."

"I love you too, sweet girl." Mama was flustering. "You're speaking! What can I get you?"

"Mama, it's time."

"What?"

"It's time." She knew Mama knew what that meant.

"No." Mama whispered. "No!"

"Mama, listen to me." Martha looked up at her father, he nodded with approval and encouragement.

"I can't lose you too!" Mama whispered.

"Mama," Martha didn't know how she knew what to say, but she did, "you're not losing me."

"I'm going to miss you so much!" Mama said, tears filling her eyes.

"I know." I'll miss you too. Martha looked up one more time at her father, as she did, he placed his right hand on Mama's cheek. Though Martha knew Mama couldn't see him or hear him, she also knew she felt something, because Mama leaned into his touch and her tears spilled over splashing on the blanket.

"Baby girl," Mama's voice was pleading, "keep fighting! You're getting stronger."

"No," Martha said with finality. "I'm not."

Mama nodded and cried harder now, holding Martha's hand tightly with both of hers. She kissed the back of Martha's hand and started shaking.

"Mama," Martha said with a tone of urgency. "Father loves you." At these words, Martha lost all control of her emotions and tears fell freely. "He always has and always will."

Mama stopped shaking and looked Martha in the eye. "What?" she asked.

Martha looked up at her father, he was crying hard now too. She didn't know how everything would work out but somehow, she knew it would. Mama looked at Martha, and followed her gaze up to Martha's left, then back to Martha.

"He's here?" Mama whispered.

"Yes." Martha said, the strength and surety in her voice calmed Mama somewhat. Still looking at her father, Martha could see how much he loved her mother. Ther was no doubt that he always had and that he deeply regretted making the mistakes he had made. She stared at him for a long time, entranced by the way he looked at Mama. Then, he looked up at the far side of the room. Martha followed his gaze and Mama followed hers. In the corner of the room stood a woman who looked so much like Mama, Martha gasped. "Aunt Angie?" The woman nodded and smiled. Martha knew Mama couldn't see her.

Mama was staring at Martha in disbelief.

"Mama," Martha said, pulling her hand from Mama's grip and pulled at Mama's curls with her fingers, like she had done when she was a little girl. "It will all be alright." Martha looked up at Aunt Agnie, who mouthed something she couldn't hear but she knew what she'd said.

"Mama," Martha said, looking at her aunt, her real aunt, "She says she told you."

"What?" Mama said, sitting up straight in her chair for the first time.

"She says, I told you Lizzie." Martha looked back at Mama. "I don't know what she's talking about, but that's what she said."

"I know." Mama said, her tears were nearly dry now.

"She loves you too." Martha conveyed for Angie.

"I know." Mama said placing her hands over her heart.

"Mama, I love you!" Martha said, reaching both arms toward her mother.

"I love you too!" Mama said, standing and leaning in to hold Martha one last time.

"We will be together again," Martha said, her voice now straining. "I promise. A real family like it was always supposed to be."

Martha gasped, Mama helped lay her back against the pillows. "I'll get Daniel." Mama said, as she let go of Martha.

"No." Martha choked. "I just want you."

"Alright." Mama said, her tears were falling in earnest. She sat back down in the chair and held Martha's hand.

"Thank you." Martha said.

"For what?" Mama asked.

"For reading me stories about Jesus." Martha replied. "For everything."

Mama didn't say anything, her tears began again, and she could only squeeze Martha's hand.

Martha looked at Mama. The reprieve was over. Her muscles began to tighten, and her nerves burned. The pain wasn't so much this time though. She looked up with her eyes, her father was holding her shoulder, he looked serene, waiting. Aunt Angie walked up to the foot of the bed now and placed both of her hands on Martha's feet. The tightness in her jaw increased, she couldn't move it much.

"I love you." She managed to whisper just as her teeth clamped shut.

"I love you!" Mama said, squeezing her hand firmly.

The tightness increased from her jaw down into her throat and her chest, there was still no pain. She couldn't breathe.

"It's time." Her father said, taking her by her perfect right hand. He pulled gently and she wanted nothing more than to go with him, she closed her eyes and allowed herself to be pulled to her feet. She turned and saw Mama holding her hand as her body lay still and lifeless in the bed. Mama cried and screamed, "NO!" As she did, the door opened, and Uncle Daniel rushed in with two nurses. Checking for vitals, then Uncle Daniel collapsed to the floor and held Mama who slid from her chair into his arms, they cried together as Martha's father led her to the foot of the bed. Aunt Angie hugged Martha tightly before the three of them left the room.

Chapter 18

The dull dimly lit hospital was a stark contrast to what she saw now. The hospital, with its large windows to let in as much light as possible, seemed so dark and dim now, though before they'd seemed almost unbearably bright at times. At night, the gas lamps the nurses lit now seemed so insufficient to see by. Everything here was light, even the people. She had thought communication couldn't have been more accessible when Uncle Daniel had had a telephone installed in the main house. But here, it was as if anyone could talk to anyone else simply by desiring to. There was so much she wouldn't have believed in her life before.

Everything was so clear and peaceful here. It all was undoubtedly real. How had Martha ever thought that death was the end of life? She felt more real now than she ever had before, more… alive. The most perfect feeling of love permeated everything she was. The colors were more vivid. There were things she understood instinctively that she never could have imagined before she had died. She had only left the hospital a few moments ago but it felt like ages. Buildings and people were everywhere, but they were more beautiful and perfect than she could have even dreamed of anything being.

There were some people who seemed to prefer to stay away from the brighter areas. The light seemed to offend them somehow. At one point, she and her father walked to the place of mist; Aunt Angie called it the shadows, but it was the same place that she had dreamed of being when she'd first met her father's mother. There was a sense of darkness in the mist, rather than actual darkness. The feeling was unmistakable and tangible. Most people within the mist seemed to instinctively move out of it and into the light. Others would inch closer to the light but then eventually withdraw further into the shadows. Others still, would stand still as if lost, until someone from the light ventured to talk to them, at which point most would follow them gratefully into the light but a few would grow angry and turn and walk purposefully into the darkness and the mist with no desire to be surrounded by this light and love that Martha had grown so accustomed to in such a short time.

Over time, Martha learned that this place was a waiting place. Where everyone who died came to wait until the great and last day. She wasn't certain what that day was yet, but she was learning. She was often with her father and her grandmother, and her Aunt Angie. Other times, she would walk alone and think and ponder the things that she had learned.

There were frequent lessons she attended, to learn more about this place, more about who she truly was. She even learned more about Jesus and God! One lesson she learned, and wasn't surprised to know, was that the life she'd led and loved with Mama was not her first life. She had existed before that, in what was referred to as the pre-existence. An existence before life as she knew it. Where she lived with others as a spirit, where she learned and grew in knowledge and favor beside God Himself, who was in very fact, the Father of her spirit. She learned that the life she had just lived, and left was given to her as a test of sorts, to allow her to choose for herself if she really wanted to continue to follow God, who she now knew as her Heavenly Father, and His plan for her, or if she would rather live a life of greed and sorrow. This gave her pause and she pondered it often. How could anyone not want to live this way, to live in this light? She understood this lesson to be accurate and true. She felt the truth of it. But she couldn't comprehend why the test of life was even necessary. It troubled her more than she wanted to admit.

It was this subject that she was contemplating one day as she walked. She came to the edge of a beautiful green field that was filled with flowers more than she could name in more colors than existed in her mortal life, when she sat upon an elegantly crafted bench. The bench faced the flowery field, but as she sat, she lifted one leg and tucked it under the other, wrapped her arm around the back of the bench and she looked and the rolling mist that looked more like a low fog from here. She knew that if she walked into it, the further she went the thicker it would become and that dark feeling of being lost would be overwhelming. She pondered about her life being a test, about how she was proving to herself more than anyone else what kind of life she wanted to lead.

As she pondered and thought about the implications of it, the big choices everyone made, she saw a man walking in the distance in the mist. She couldn't make out his features, but she could tell he was walking slowly. There were people around her walking on the grass or the paths. Others were walking so quickly they were certainly busy with important matters, but this man was barely moving in comparison. He would take one slow step towards the break in the mist, one step closer to the open flowery field and all the love and light anyone could hope for, then he would inch back and pause. He'd take another step slowly and inch back again. He did this multiple times before he came to a standstill and collapsed to the ground in indecision. She could feel his discouragement from here. As she watched the man, movement to her right caught her eye. Another man was walking slowly but with purpose from the field into the mist. As he did so, the first man lifted his head and watched the second man as he approached. She couldn't hear the words they exchanged but the second man helped the first into a standing position and they embraced. After they released each other, the second man was animated as he spoke to the first man, she could feel his excitement and enthusiasm as he relayed his message to the first man. The first man was no longer full of discouragement though indecision still flooded him. The second man pointed towards the field and the first man nodded. The first man seemed to beam with joy that nearly overwhelmed her, then he wrapped his arm around the first man's shoulders, and they walked toward the edge of the mist.

As they approached and the mist thinned, she could see an uncanny resemblance between the two men, they must be brothers if not twins. The second man was bursting with joy and hope and love, and while the first man clearly cared for the second man, he was visibly uncomfortable. He squinted as they stepped out of the mist, and he curled his body back slightly. The second man let go of the first man's shoulders and stood to face his brother. She still couldn't hear what was being said, but words wouldn't tell her more than she could see firsthand. Slowly, and almost imperceptibly, as if he didn't realize he was even doing it, the first man inched closer and closer to the mist. The second man stood his ground but kept conversing with the first man. The closer the first man got to the shadows the more at ease he seemed to be, more comfortable. More relaxed. Not happy, but it was familiar to him. The second man stood still, stopped talking, and once he wiped a tear from his face, both brothers lifted their arms in a farewell and the first man turned, and walked purposefully back into the shadowy mist all indecision gone.

"It's hard to watch, isn't it?" Martha turned to see her father standing behind her. He'd asked the question, though she knew it wasn't a question really.

"It is." She answered.

"I know you were wondering why we needed to go through the life test, does it make more sense now?"

"I think so," She said, "but in some ways it still doesn't make sense. Why wouldn't God just make us choose so we could all enjoy this!

"When that man first walked out of the shadows, did he look like he was enjoying it?" Her father asked.

"No." Martha admitted. "He looked very unhappy and uncomfortable."

"And that's why we go through the life test. Not everyone wants to live in the light. Some prefer the shadows." He then sat down next to her on the bench.

Martha turned and faced the field now, her father next to her, they both looked forward. "This is all so much to take in!" She sighed.

"It really is." He admitted.

"How many people choose the shadows over the light?" she asked.

"Not many." He said. "But enough to make it vitally important that the choice be theirs."

"Wouldn't even one person be enough for that to be important?"

"Exactly." He stood and started walking away. "Come with me, I want to show you something."

"Where are we going?" she asked.

"Somewhere familiar and, new at the same time." He paused, then turned and looked at her, "Be prepared though, it will feel very strange the first time." He held out his hand for her to follow him.

As she held his hand and took a few steps, but suddenly they were somewhere else, and the flowery field was nowhere in sight. They stood at the edge of a road. The weather was peaceful and the grass on either side of the road was green. There were trees sprawling across the ground and the road welcomed travelers who passed under a large stone archway. The main arch was taller than she could reach standing on her tiptoes, while two smaller arches joined the center on either side, wide enough for a large man to walk through comfortably. The top of the arch wall was flat and boasted large spheres on the tops of the four supporting pillars that separated the three arches. There was a carved inscription at the top, it read, "Oakwood Cemetery".

"Oh." She gasped. As they walked under the main arch a strange sensation washed over her. She knew why they were here, though she had never thought of visiting it before. They walked on the dirt road that wound around a few curves. Martha had never cared for cemeteries when she was alive, and now that she was no longer, it felt even stranger to be in one. Her father led the way down one road to another joining one, then another. She had been here only once before, and that was on the day of her burial, she had to be there for Mama's sake. She felt that her presence then had meant something to her mother even if she hadn't been able to see her.

They walked around one last corner, and there in front of her was the strangest sight she'd ever seen. A headstone that stood to Martha's waist, inscribed thereon: "Martha 'Mary' Rose Hart, Born Jun. 26, 1908, Died Nov. 2, 1922"

"When?" Martha asked. She hadn't even thought about there being a headstone here. Maybe she'd known about it, but why would she think about it? She knew she was dead, but it felt so much more like living.

"About six months ago." He answered.

"A year after?" she asked.

Her father nodded, "They placed the stone almost exactly a year after your passing."

They walked around and after a while her father left her alone there. It had taken Martha some time to process the idea of this knew state of being. She had learned so much and understood it all to be true. But emotionally, she still felt she was coming around to the idea of everything. She comprehended everything she learned but her emotions were so much stronger now that sometimes it felt harder to accept change than it had in life. Everything she had hoped for and loved and enjoyed while she was alive, she still very much loved and enjoyed and hoped for, and if possible, more than she had before.

"OH!" Dawning clicked and she was able to align her understanding to the emotion. She found her father sitting on the bench he'd found her on before they went to the cemetery. He was talking to one of their teachers; Martha and her father had taken a lot of their lessons together as he had learned some things before she had died, but he wanted to join her since he couldn't progress yet. It was wonderful to be able to have him there and offer his insight and opinions on different subjects, especially when she'd had questions. They had a few different teachers but the man talking with Father now was one of her favorites.

Martha walked slowly as she approached the bench so as not to interrupt their conversation. As she got closer, the teacher waved and bid farewell to her father.

"I understand now," she said, "about why some people choose to go and stay in the shadows."

"Do you?" he asked, a smile played at the corner of his mouth.

"Yes!" She said, feeling giddy with the excitement of making the deep emotional connection to this clearly important lesson. "In life, we experience new things, things we couldn't experience without our bodies, and those things we experienced allowed us to form preferences that aligned with our unique individuality."

"Go on." He urged; he seemed to appreciate her take on it.

"Before we were born, it was easy for us to say that we wanted what God wanted because He only had what He wanted for us. We didn't know any different." She said, feeling satisfied with her answer.

"And?" Her father encouraged her, apparently, he was not satisfied.

"And…" She thought for a moment, allowing her emotions to fully connect with the understanding. "And unless we were completely separated from Him, forgetting about Him entirely, we would never be able to form our own opinions, our own preferences. We wouldn't have been able to fully grow our emotional side."

"That is very profound." he said, mulling over what she had just said. "I'd never quite thought if it like that before."

"So, when people choose the shadow over the light, it's not a containment for them, it's a feeling of comfort and familiarity, isn't it." She said, sitting and contemplating on the gravity of this revelation.

"Yes." He said.

Martha glanced at him, a tear filled his eye, and he wiped it away before it fell, but emotions here were strong; they emanated from everyone as clearly as words. He was grieving, a great loss.

"Do you think we would even know what loss feels like if we had never been alive?" She asked him.

"No." he said simply, allowing the grief to sit for a minute, he wanted to feel it for now, he welcomed it.

"Wouldn't that have been a good thing?" She said, trying to comprehend why he wanted to feel so sad when he didn't have to.

"If we never knew grief and pain, that also means we never knew real joy or happiness," he said simply, "and that means we never would have been truly happy, ever, for all eternity."

She pondered that and realized that was what the life test was really for. "So," she said, "For us to discover happiness and sadness and experiment for ourselves where on that emotional scale we were truly comfortable most of the time. That's what the test was. It wasn't so much of us being tested, but we were testing ourselves. A sort of experiment for us to discover who we really were without His constant presence and influence in our lives."

He nodded. "I think you have that down."

"Who are you grieving?" she asked without looking at him.

"My father." He said simply. Without further words, he stood, turned, and looked at the misty shadows, staring at them for only a moment, then let the grief melt away before looking at her. As he smiled, looking into her eyes, she felt such a wave of love and joy roll off him that she could only breathe it in and smile back. Then he turned and walked away.

Martha visited the cemetery where her body was buried often, she wasn't sure why. There was comfort to it, she supposed. The first time Martha saw Suzie at the cemetery was two years after Martha's first visit here. Suzie had come to the cemetery to visit her father's grave. Martha had watched her as she laid flowers next to her father's headstone, tears had filled Suzie's eyes, and she had cried for a long time. Then she talked with him, he was there too, though Suzie couldn't see him. Martha kept her distance; she didn't want to intrude on their private moment. Suzie's father waved at Martha, and she waved back, then Suzie finished speaking and Suzie's father touched her on the shoulder. Martha smiled, knowing that Suzie felt something, that Suzie knew she wasn't alone. After Suzie's father had left, Suzie stayed at his graveside for a few minutes before Suzie got up and walked toward Martha. Martha was touched when Suzie stopped at her grave.

"Hi, Mary." Suzie said.

"Hello, my sweet friend." Martha replied, knowing Suzie couldn't hear her.

"I just finished visiting my father, and remembered you were here too, so I thought I'd come and talk with you for a while." Suzie sat on the grass facing Martha's headstone.

"I'm glad you did." Martha whispered, taking a seat on the grass next to Suzie.

"I'm sorry I didn't think to bring you flowers too." Suzie said, shedding a single tear before wiping it away.

"You never have to." Martha tried to impress on Suzie.

"I'll have to remember to come visit you from time to time too, just like I do my father. I come here on his birthday and on the day he died every year." Suzie paused, deep in thought.

"That's very thoughtful." Martha said.

"Mother used to come, for the first couple of years. I think it made her more sad though, so she stopped coming. I know she hasn't forgotten him, but I do miss coming with her."

Martha didn't respond this time.

"I miss having our family together, Mary. I think, looking back, that's when I started being mean to people, when Mother stopped coming to the cemetery with me. I think I felt like I was losing my family and there was no way I could control it. It hurt and it scared me to think I was losing my mother too."

Martha felt deeply pained for her friend's grief and fear.

"Being angry hurt less than being scared and sad."

Martha wished she could tell Suzie all that she knew now, how families could go on even after death. That losing her father in this life wasn't the end. That they could truly be a family forever. Her, her father and her mother. She had never wished for anything more in her existence.

"Thank you, Mary." Suzie said after a long pause. "I never had a friend like you, I only wish I'd gotten to know you better before you died. I miss having a friend like you."

"Isn't May still your friend?" Martha asked, hoping to get an answer to the question she knew Suzie couldn't hear.

"I still see May at school, but I think she's shut down quite a bit since you passed too. Nothing is quite the same without you here."

Martha's heart broke a little. She knew her friends and family would be alright, but it was so hard watching them without being able to do much to help them.

"I miss you, Mary." Suzie wiped another tear from her eye. "I miss you and my father."

Martha wished she could just wrap her arms around Suzie, the way that Suzie had done for her so many unexpected times in the short span of their friendship.

"I think I'm a better person because of you, you know." Suzie said, standing from the ground. "You knew what I needed when I needed it. Maybe I'll try to help May the way you helped me."

Martha stood and threw her arms around her friend, even though Suzie couldn't feel it or see her, she wanted Suzie to know she cared and was grateful. Suzie breathed deeply and started crying without restraint. Martha pulled away and Suzie put her hands over her heart.

"I love you too, Martha." Suzie said and she walked away.

Maybe Martha had more influence than she had thought she had.

Martha left the cemetery and found her father deep in thought on a mountain side. She relayed everything she had seen and heard at the cemetery, and he simply laughed.

"You didn't think we had any influence at all?"

"I hadn't thought about it." Martha admitted. "I don't have a body anymore and no one can see or hear me. Now that I know it though, it seems silly that I hadn't known."

"So, all those nights we talked before you died didn't give you a clue?" He laughed again.

"Oh!" She said stunned. She hadn't thought about that since she had died.

"What?" He asked, sincerity in voice as well as humor.

"I kept thinking that those were just dreams." she admitted.

"They were dreams, but really me and your grandmother visiting you in your dreams."

"Huh." was all she could think of to say in response.

"You can probably guess that it's usually easier to impress upon a subconscious mind than a fully conscious one by now." He said, watching her to see when she made the connection.

"Usually?" she asked.

"Yes, usually." He said, looking away from her and off in the distance. "After your mother left me, she had a sort of faith crisis."

"She did?" Martha asked. "I knew she stopped reading her Bible after Aunt Angie died, but I didn't think there was more to lose after that."

"Yes, and I'm afraid I was largely to blame." he said as he sat forward, pulling his legs up and resting his arms on his knees. "She was in a very unsafe situation before we married, ever since her sister, your Aunt Angie died. When we got married, we were so happy, and in a large way our marriage saved your mother. I took her away from all that pain and grief she'd known for years. When we first married, she loved God. She was a good person and lived by faith so strongly, even through all the trials she went through, she never doubted that God existed and that He was watching over her. She prayed daily and thanked Him for everything continually, especially for me. So even though she didn't read her bible anymore. And she still sometimes blamed God for the bad things that happened, she still believed in him." He paused and wiped his tears. "After she left me though, to keep you safe, and rightly so, her faith faltered. She stopped praying. Stopped talking about God and never mentioned any of that to you. Until you were in the hospital anyway."

Martha thought about this for a while, and at length asked, "How does Mama's faith crisis tie in to impressing on people?"

"You see, if someone believes in God and they're watching for signs after they already have faith, it's easier to help them feel our presence. It's easier for them to feel the influence of the Holy Spirit and to recognize promptings and impressions that come, even if they're fully awake. If someone doubts, or doesn't believe at all, most of the time no matter how hard we try, the message never comes through. If someone, like you, doesn't really know either way what to believe or not believe, the subconscious may be easier to reach."

"So, Suzie could feel my presence there, even though she couldn't see or hear me, because she had purposely gone

to the cemetery in hopes that there is more after death?"
Martha guessed.

"I believe so." He answered. "You told me she was talking to you and her father, correct?"

"Yes," Martha replied.

"Even if she doesn't admit it out loud or even to herself, she wouldn't go to the cemetery to talk to her deceased loved ones if she didn't think on some level they could hear her." He stood after saying this. "That would be insanity."

A brief memory flashed across Martha's mind as she watched her father walk down the steep side of the mountain without a struggle.

"Father!" She called after him.

He stopped and turned, "Yes?"

"I just remembered that Mama once said you had a limp and a severe stutter." She said, questioning.

He hesitated, then looked down at his legs, jumped a couple of times then looked back at Martha. He ran back up the slope with ease. When he reached her again, he faced her, smiled sincerely, then quickly grabbed both of her arms, and waved them in front of her face.

"And YOU were supposed to only have one hand!" He laughed loudly then ran at full speed down the side of the mountain and didn't stop laughing even after he'd left earshot.

She looked down at her hands, both perfectly formed and intact. Maybe she hadn't noticed because the bandage around her amputation hadn't been removed before she had died, so she had never had to get used to only having one hand.

She supposed she should have thought of that. She laughed and followed his carefree path down the mountain, enjoying the exhilarating run.

After that, Suzie kept her word and visited Martha's gravesite regularly. Martha always met her there. Martha listened to Suzie talk about her life and her wishes and dreams. One day, she told Martha about her new baby girl, whom she'd named after her.

"I wanted you to know, that we named her Mary Sue." Suzie said, and Martha's heart filled to the brim with joy and love for her friend. Suzie caught Martha up on all that had happened over the last few months, and when she had finished talking, she stood, said goodbye and left to return home to her new baby.

Martha sat for a while longer, then felt a firm hand on her shoulder. She hadn't heard anyone approaching she'd been in such deep thought. She looked up and saw her father standing there, she loved seeing his beautiful blue eyes smiling down at her, today they seemed brighter than ever.

"It's time." Was all he said.

Martha took his hand as her father helped her stand, and they walked off together, hand in hand.

"It's been a long time." Martha said as they walked through the main entrance. It wasn't at all necessary, they could have simply entered directly into the room they intended to go to, but it felt right to walk through the front doors today.

"It has been." Her father said.

"Was it hard when you came for me?" Martha asked.

"Why would it be hard?" he asked.

"Seeing me like that." She said, clarifying, "as I was dying."

"No." he answered. "It wasn't hard. I didn't enjoy seeing you suffer day after day. But the day we came to greet you was one of the best days I can remember. I was welcoming my daughter into my arms for the first time."

"I can't wait to see her and talk to her again. It's been so long." Martha said. "And not so long at the same time."

Martha and her father walked through the hallways of the hospital, the same hospital that Martha had stayed in for the last days of her mortal existence. She was amazed and not surprised at how many other people she saw there, waiting to collect their loved ones who were passing on from their lives. She knew some of them by name, others she recognized by appearance only. They continued to walk down the hallways navigating past doors and nurses. They finally approached the room they were looking for and entered.

Mama lay there, sleeping in her hospital bed. A mask covered her mouth and nose; a tube connected to the mask delivered oxygen to her. As she slept, her breathing was shallow and raspy. Father was right, it was hard to see the suffering, but she was very excited to hug her again. As Martha watched, Mama's breath grew more shallow and raspy by the minute. Mama had been admitted to the hospital only a few days ago when a case of pneumonia made it difficult to breathe. She was so beautiful there, her curly hair, now completely gray. Her face was worn from time and experience, each wrinkle a testament to the life she'd lived. Most of her wrinkles came from laughter or worry. Mama was truly a woman who cared and loved deeply. Martha wondered why Mama had never remarried and often hoped she would have gone back to California after the death of her daughter and confirmation that her husband had passed, but here Mama had stayed, taking care of the Ruth, Daniel, and their children as best she knew how. Now, she was being cared for by others here until the end.

Father approached the bed and whispered something in Mama's ear that Martha couldn't hear. Mama's eyes flashed open, her breathing stronger, if only just.

"Will?" Mama whispered as tears streamed down her face.

Father nodded and held her hand. He pulled her to standing and they embraced for a long time, Mama's frail looking body lay there on the bed as she stood, her youthful, strong arms wrapped around her husband for the first time in nearly forty years. They held each other oblivious to Mama's roommate alerting nurses that Mama had stopped breathing; unaware of the medical staff that hurried around her to check for vitals and see what they could do to help. As a doctor called time of death, Mama finally turned and looked at Martha. They hugged each other for only a moment before father stepped next to them and wrapped them both in his big, strong arms.

Chapter 19

Amanda lifted the last file box from the back of her white Nissan Sentra and Jason closed the trunk.

"Are you sure you don't want me to carry that for you?" He said. He was always so chivalrous.

"No," Amanda declined his help. "If you could feed Cayson lunch for me, that would help a lot. I'd love to get started on a couple of boxes to just see what Grandma had! I don't have a clue what any of this is but I'm seriously so excited."

"Alright." Jason laughed as followed Amanda up the steps.

Jason opened the front door for Amanda and closed it behind them when they were both inside. She walked straight to the stairs and saw Jason pick up Cayson from his playpen just as she disappeared from their view. All the file boxes from Grandma's house were piled haphazardly in the corner of the basement now. She knew she wouldn't be able to do much tonight but also knew that if she waited even until morning, she would lose her momentum and not be able to find the time or desire to start. IF she could just look through a couple of these boxes, she may be able to pique her interest enough to carry her for the next few days.

She sat cross-legged on the floor and opened the box she had just carried down the stairs. At the top of the box, the first thing she saw was a letter. A letter addressed to William Hart. She felt drawn to it, and when she read it, she cried.

She finished the letter and closed the box and ran upstairs so quickly into the kitchen that Jason was visibly concerned.

"Are you ok?" He asked, holding a spoon full of baby food midair, just far enough from a baby Cayson's flailing arms that their son was getting frustrated about his dinner being interrupted.

"Jason!" Amanda half shouted startling Cayson out of his frustration.

"Is there a spider or a dead mouse in one of those boxes you need me to take care of?" His joking tone made her smile.

"No!" she said, "But if I find one, you know I'll scream for you." She laughed with him for a moment.

Jason fed the bite to Cayson and pressed, "What happened?"

"Do you remember that relative I found? Elizabeth Loudry?"

"Was she the one that Married, who was it… something Heath?"

"Willima Hart." She corrected.

"That's right." He said, feeding another bite to the baby in the highchair who was growing impatient that his bites were coming too slowly for his liking. "Didn't she disappear, and no one knew what happened to her?"

"YES!" Amanda said, jumping up and down, she could hardly contain her excitement. "I found her!"

"You already found her, Amanda, we did her work didn't we?"

"Yes. We did" Amanda said. A huge smile spread across her face. "But not all of it!"

"Yes, we did! We did her sealing last month, didn't we?" He asked.

"We did, to her husband Will, but not to their daughter!" She said in a half whisper yell. It all felt conspiratorial.

"WHAT?!" Jason said, dropping the spoon full of food onto the highchair tray and walking over to Amanda.

"They had a daughter." Amanda said.

"How do you know?" Jason asked. She knew he wasn't nearly as interested in family history and genealogy as she was but bless this man for matching her energy when she needed him to.

"I opened one of those boxes from my grandmother's house and right at the top there was a letter!" She said animatedly miming opening the box and finding it.

"A letter?" Jason was no longer just matching her energy; he was truly invested now.

"Yes. A letter from Elizabeth to William, AFTER she disappeared." She was getting so excited she was becoming dizzy. She crossed the room to sit at the table next to the highchair and Jason followed taking his post as baby feeder again.

"What did the letter say?" Jason encouraged her to continue.

"It was Elizabeth explaining to William why she left. That she had a baby and told him he had a daughter! She left to keep her safe, I'm not sure what she was keeping them safe from, but they had a daughter! I need to find more so I can claim her too!" Amanda was bouncing in her seat from the excitement. "I bet there's more about them in those boxes, Jason. I just know it!"

"You're probably right, but it's late and you need dinner and sleep."

Amanda agreed and made a quick dinner of chicken and rice for Jason and herself as Jason finished feeding Cayson and got him ready for bed. The couple ate dinner then went to bed themselves.

The next morning, they woke up, had breakfast then all went down to the basement. Jason worked in the office corner; they were so blessed he could work from home most of the time. Cayson got set up in his little play area next to the desk. Amanda went straight to the corner with all the boxes and opened the one that she had found the letter in. There were more letters from Elizabeth to William, but also to her brother. Then she found everything she needed about Elizabeth and William's daughter, Martha Rose Hart.

She took the next few days adding everything she had to the online database she was using to create the personal file for this new relative that no one knew existed before. She scanned images of the letters and even the birth certificate she had found and uploaded them to the website. She connected Martha's profile to her parents, then continued for the next few days digging for more information on Martha.

After a few boxes and more than a week of looking, Amanda finally found the death certificate for Martha. She was so young! Only about 14 years old. Amanda's heart ached for her, her long lost cousin. Did she have anyone other than her mother to care for her? Were she and Elizabeth all alone for fourteen years? She scanned in and uploaded the death certificate for Martha then created a temple file for her.

Amanda had only been working on Martha's history for a couple of weeks but already felt closer to her than she had felt to anyone else she had done work for. She and Jason arranged to have Jason's mother watch Cayson so that the couple could go to the temple next month to do the baptisms for Martha as well as Martha's grandfather, William's father. She wasn't sure why they hadn't done his work yet, but they were both excited to be able to do this for their family who couldn't do it for themselves.

The day finally came. They dropped Cayson off at his grandmother's house and they went on to the temple. The spire greeted them as they approached the parking lot, once they got out of the car and started walking toward the temple, an immense sense of peace flooded Amanda and she was grateful for this opportunity to serve Martha, whom she had never met, but knew she loved dearly.

They walked in front of the large reflection pool in front of the main temple doors at the front of the building and they paused and took a picture together in front of it.

"I wish I could find a photo of Martha." Amanda said, "I wonder what she looked like."

They moved on and Jason opened the door for Amanda. They entered the beautiful ornate building and once more, Amanda paused.

"Are you alright?" Jason asked.

"Yes, I just need a moment." Tears welled in her eyes, and she felt as though she needed to take a deep breath and just prepare herself for this sacred event.

They stood in the entryway of the temple, a few people came and passed them, a couple going down to the baptistry, but most going to the main temple. Amanda just stood there, calm and peaceful. The anticipation of the moment building and she hoped that Martha was just as excited as she was! Amanda felt a serene smile spread across her face, and she knew Martha was close by. A tear escaped and rolled down her cheek. Her smile broadened with knowing.

"Are you ready?" Jason asked. Amanda was speechless. She nodded and the couple walked down the marble stairway together.

At the bottom of the stairway, they approached a desk, and Amanda and Jason both scanned their recommend cards. They got their baptismal whites, jump suits that they would wear to be baptized for their ancestors in. After Amanda changed, she walked back into the chapel that was adjacent to the room where they scanned at the desk. She breathed deeply as she waited for Jason to come back and sit with her. After he changed, he came out to the chapel and joined her, as he took her hand in his, he lifted her fingers to his mouth and rested the softest kiss there before he grasped her hand tightly with both of his. Another tear rolled down her cheek and she couldn't explain the love and hope she felt. There were no words. Jason didn't need an explanation though. He just sat next to her, holding her one hand in both of his in his lap, his head bowed, and his eyes closed in silent reverence and prayer. She stared in front of her, at the windows that separated the benches of the chapel from the font. She watched a group of girls, around the age Martha was when she died, taking turns being baptized for others who also had passed on from this life. She watched as, one girl came up out of the water and walked up the stairs of the large font, and another girl walked down into the warm water waiting for her. The man in the water that was performing the baptism, held out his hand to her to help her balance as she walked to him in the water that came up past her waist.

The man held his right arm to side, and she held his other arm for balance. He said a few words which Amanda couldn't hear from this side of the glass, but she knew them by heart. The baptismal prayer. Then, when the man was finished speaking, he lowered his right arm, and placed his hand on the girl's upper back, and guided her completely under the water, then brought her right back up.

"Is this your whole group?" A man in an all-white suit whispered to Jason, who nodded in the affirmative. They were ushered back to the font room. Amanda walked through the women's changing room and Jason through the men's. They met again on the large platform that held a small computer on one side with a simple desk and chair, as two benches along the back side by the wall. A metal handrail with glass panels underneath separated the platform from a sudden drop off; there was a break in the center of the railing and glass panels for the stairs that led directly into the font. Amanda peered over the edge of one side of the railing to see the bottom of the font, where stood, on an intricate marble floor, twelve stone oxen held the large basin of water that was the font, on their backs.

Amanda looked down at her hand where she held the piece of paper that meant everything for Martha. It had only Martha's name, her birth date and place and the day she died. She watched Jason step down into the water, and when he was in the center of the water, he turned and silently held out his hand to Amanda, beckoning her to him. She took a deep breath and smiled. Then handed the small piece of paper to the man in another white suit, who was sitting at the small desk, and followed her beloved husband into the water. Jason held her hand and guided her to him, she held his left wrist with her left hand, and with his left hand held her right wrist. He then raised his right arm behind her.

"Sister Jenson, I baptize you for and in behalf of Martha Rose Hart."

Chapter 20

Martha stood on the platform and watched as Jason took Amanda by the hand guided her into the water. A few tears had fallen consistently since she entered the temple with her mother, father and Amanda. But when she heard Jason call her name, the tears were uncontrollable. The joy and peace she immediately felt was like nothing she had ever experienced in her whole life or afterlife.

"Amen." Jason finished the covenantal prayer, and he held Amanda so steadily as he helped her go under the water completely then back up to a standing position. Martha was overwhelmed with gratitude and love for this woman. Her cousin, who would do this for her.

"Do you accept her proxy baptism as your own?" A kind and gentle voice beside her asked. It was her teacher.

"Yes!" She said turning to him, he smiled, and wrote something down in his notebook, then closed it and gave her a big hug. They cried together only for a moment before he released her and Martha hugged her parents in turn.

Martha watched as Amanda climbed out of the water.

"Thank you!" Martha said, she embraced Amanda just as a woman wrapped a towel around her. Amand burst into tears, and she didn't seem to mind.

The woman who had handed the towel to Amanda smiled, and shed a tear too as she said, "She's here. She's been waiting a long time for this."

"I know." Amanda smiled with her reply.

"I'm so grateful for you and I love you, Amanda." Martha said, knowing that she couldn't hear her, but also knowing she knew.

Chapter 21

As Martha climbed the basement stairs with the photograph in hand. She smiled again at the memory of Amanda taking her name to the temple and being baptized for her. She looked down at the picture. It was a printed copy of an older photograph. But the image was so clear.

There she was, a young Martha, before she knew about her father. Before she felt she had no one. Before all the heartache and pain. The only picture she had ever been in, Mama hadn't wanted photos taken of either herself or Martha to protect them both. Just one more thing that, now, Martha understood was her mother's way of showing such deep love for her. But this day, had been different. It had been Martha's birthday and Mama had decided that they needed one photograph together. They were sitting in their small sitting room in the front of their tiny house. Happy. Loved. Content. How had things changed so much in such a short time all those years ago? She placed the photo on the shelf at the top of the stairs. This was what she had come here for. This picture was what she had come to help Amanda find.

Martha left the house and walked down the street towards the beautiful sunset feeling content, happy, belonging, loved and finally, claimed!